MW00929300

Addicted To Loving A Boss 3

Copyright 2017

Instagram: MSTJADAMS
Twitter: jenkinstina72
Facebook: Author T Jenkins

This novel is a work of fiction. Any resemblances to actual events, real people, living or dead, organizations, establishments or locales are products of the author's imagination. Other names, characters, places, and incidents are used fictionally.

All parts reserved. No part of this book may be used or reproduced in any form or by any means electronic or mechanical, including photocopying, recording or by information storage and retrieval system, without written permission from the publisher and write.

Because of the dynamic nature of the Internet, any web address or links contained in this book may have changed since publication, and may no longer be valid.

More books from me:

The Thug I Chose 1, 2 & 3
A Thin Line Between Me and My Thug 1 & 2
I Got Luv For My Shawty 1 & 2
Kharis and Caleb: A Different Kind of Love 1 & 2
Loving You Is A Battle 1 & 2 & 3
Violet and The Connect 1 & 2 & 3
You Complete Me
Love Will Lead You Back
This Thing Called Love
Are We In This Together 1 & 2
Shawty Down To Ride For a Boss 1 & 2
When A Boss Falls in Love 1, 2 & 3
Let Me Be The One 1 & 2
We Got That Forever Love
Aint No Savage Like The One I Got 1&2
A Queen and A Hustla 1&2
Thirsty For A Bad Boy 1&2
Hassan and Serena: An Unforgettable Love 1&2
Caught up Luvin A Beast 1, 2 & 3
A Street King and His Shawty 1 & 2

Birch

I really wanted to see Isa at the baby shower but after Maylan told me her and Vernon had it out, I knew it wasn't happening. She said he wasn't disrespectful and I knew that already because he told me everything. I don't know why the hell she snapped on him but missing her best friends baby shower is shady if you ask me. That's like me and one of my boys not talking but they're having something for their kids, I'm still pulling up.

Lira only came because my ass was being lazy and didn't feel like dropping her off. We had gone to the movies and she lived out of the way from where Maylan lived and I was already running late. Dawn and Maylan gave her dirty looks the entire time but she knew not to say anything. Lique is one person she could talk shit to all she wanted but Vernon and Dante would never let it go down with their women. I wouldn't with Isa either but she wasn't here so it didn't matter.

After the baby shower I did take Lira home and release some stress in her mouth. She wanted to have sex but as of lately I haven't been feeling her like that. Lira wanted something I couldn't give her and that was a relationship. The only person who could ever get one out of me is Isa. Say what you want but I definitely loved her and if she called me today and said she wanted to work it out, I'd drop Lira and the stripper I was fucking in a heartbeat. Oh yea, I still had my doggish ways about me but make no mistake; Isa is the only woman I won't cheat on.

"What the hell you in here daydreaming about?" Vernon and Dante came busting through my office door. I started to yell at my secretary but what for? They always walked past her.

"Yo, has either of your women spoken to Isa?" They both shrugged their shoulders and Dante asked me why.

"It's been two days since the shower and my mom has had the kids ever since. Don't get me wrong, she loves them but Isa hasn't called or stopped by to check. It's not like her to do that.

"Maybe she needs a break. Katarina bad as hell and Abel ain't too far behind her."

"Yo don't talk about my kids like that."

"Hell no Birch them some bad motherfuckers and they learning that shit from Brayden little ass. I don't care what you say."

4

Vernon said making us all laugh.

"What the fuck ever. Why y'all ignorant niggas here anyway?"

"Ugh my office is down the hall."

"Yea but you're never in it." I told him and he waved me off to use the bathroom.

"We came by to see if you wanted to step out for a few and have drinks. It's been a while since we've all been out."

"Why not? It's only six which means the broke bitches won't be there with their hand out for free drinks until at least ten." We laughed and headed out after I locked up.

My secretary must've left right after they came. She is deathly afraid of Vernon for some reason and Dante harassed her about getting him something to drink and stupid shit like that whenever he came. The bar wasn't packed just like I knew it wouldn't be but the strippers were still working and some of the men were going in the back. Smitty and Barry came strolling in not too long after and sat down.

"I'm making a toast." It just like Barry's over educated ass to do a damn toast. We had the bartender make us all a Hennessy shot first.

"I'm making a toast to five niggas who grew up in the hood but made it out and living the American dream. We could've gotten caught up in the street life but we beat the odds. To us, our women and kids." We all let our glasses touch and tossed our drinks back.

"Hey baby can I take you in the back for some fun?" The stripper chick asked me. She and I had been getting it in but it wasn't happening tonight. I had no condoms and a nigga didn't trust the ones in the dispenser. Say what you want but those dispensers will pop open if you hit it the right way and I can't take the chance of any of them having a hole in it.

"No thanks. I got you tomorrow tho." I smacked her ass and watched it jiggle as she stepped away. Her pussy was definitely good but as I said before I'm not feeling the sex with anyone but Isa.

"What Maylan? I can barely hear you." I heard Vernon yelling in the phone and he was covering his other ear.

"I got to go y'all. I'm not sure what's going on but Maylan crying and no one is at the house with her. I want to say she's in labor but because I can't make out what she's saying I can't be sure." He snatched his keys up and we all followed behind him. He was flying in and out of traffic and all of us were right behind him. We got to the house and saw Celeste standing there with a grin on her face. Vernon damn near jumped out his car before it stopped.

"What the fuck you doing here Celeste? You good May?" He lifted her face and wiped the tears.

"Vernon I was trying to tell you I'm in pain and need to get to the hospital. I didn't know she was out here until I opened the door just now. Why is she here? Oh Godddddd." Maylan screamed and bent down holding her stomach.

"Lets go May. You say you're in labor but it looks like something else is wrong." He helped her in the car and left Celeste standing there. Vernon looked nervous as hell and he should be because his ass is about to witness a miracle. Dante locked his house up and stood behind me questioning why she was there.

"I see he's still with her. I just came to tell him the day he whooped my ass he killed the baby in my stomach." Dante and I looked at each other and then back at her.

"Bitch you know he would never run up in you raw." Dante said staring her up and down.

"Nope but I damn sure knew how to poke holes. See I know how bad he wants kids and I would've loved to see his face when he found out he killed one." I couldn't deny anything she was saying because Vernon was going to be on one when he found out.

"Instead he's running off to save that bitch once again."

"Why she got to be all that? I know you're upset he didn't choose you but she didn't make his decision." I told her.

"Do me a favor and give him this paperwork. It's from the emergency room stating I was four months." I scanned the paper and looked back up at her. Dante took it out my hand to scan it.

"I know funny right. I didn't even know and I damn sure didn't want to be a mother but something about losing a child does a number on you, regardless. Tell him good luck with his kid." She wiped the two tears that fell and got in the car to leave. I would feel bad for her but because its her I can't. If she didn't lose the baby, there's no doubt in my mind she would've reeked havoc in Vernon's relationship with Maylan.

"Yooooo, Vernon is going to have a fit."

"Yea well he won't know until after Maylan has the baby. He doesn't need anymore stress." Dante and I drove to the hospital and went to the labor and delivery floor. Vernon was pacing outside the room and said they had to give her a needle in her back and he couldn't watch. Evidently she was almost ten centimeters already.

"Yo who this?" I answered my phone without looking.

"Brayden." My stomach got butterflies in it when I heard her voice. I know I told her not to speak to me again but her voice did something to me.

"Isa."

"Yea it's me."

"Where have you been?"

"Brayden I can't talk long but can you come get me?"

"Yea where are you?" She didn't say anything.

"Isa where am I picking you up from?" Vernon and Dante stared at me. The doctor came out asking him to come in the room because Maylan was about to start pushing.

"ISA!" I yelled to get her to answer.

"JAIL BIRCH. I'M IN JAIL!

7

Birch

I paced the floor waiting for them to process Isa and bring her out. Her bail was one million dollars. When she called to inform me of her incarceration, I was shocked but in a way expected it. I'm not sure what she's in here for but nine times out of ten it has everything to do with Abel. The detective on the case wouldn't give me any information so I put a call out to Will, who is the detective that told me about them looking into Abel in the first place. Unfortunately, he's on vacation so I'm not going to find out much right now.

As I waited, all I could think about was Isa being in jail and if anything happened to her. She is a good girl with some self-esteem issues but nothing she's done in life should land her in jail. She didn't know how to fight and I was worried about her defending herself. I was seriously contemplating on teaching her. Then again, I didn't want her fighting, but fuck it.

My mom called me a hundred times asking about her release and Dawn came down once she heard. Smitty and Maria were on the way and Dante stayed on the phone speaking to Barry, who was in California. A lawyer walked up and had us follow him to a room where Isa was sitting in a chair. She ran straight to me and jumped in my arms. She was shaking uncontrollably and her cries were tearing me up on the inside.

"Brayden I should've listened to you." I moved the hair out of her face.

"What are you talking about? What happened?" I checked her over.

"I didn't know Brayden. I swear I didn't." I wiped her face with my shirt.

"I don't mean to break this up but I want to get her out of here as soon as possible. The charges are outrageous because we know she had nothing to do with it but it was her apartment." The lawyer said.

We all sat down listening to him mention kingpin charges, intent to distribute, endangering the welfare of a child and the list went on. Isa had at least ten charges against her by the time he finished. It didn't matter because like he said we all knew she wasn't a part of it. However, because she was the only one home when the raid took place, it's on her. The cops tried to get Isa to say whose drugs they were but she refused.

8

"This will be a very difficult case to beat if Ms. Harrison doesn't want to say who the drugs and weapons belonged to. I'm not saying I can't do it but she may do some time. This is her first time being in trouble so it may be no longer than three years, at the most."

"I can't go to jail Brayden. Oh my God, your mom must think I'm dumb and my babies probably think I left them. How could I be so stupid?"

She started punching herself in the head. Dawn and Maria, who had just gotten here with Smitty, sat there crying and my boys were shaking their heads. We knew it was a possibility she'd get caught up but to see it happened is crazy.

"Stop it Isa." I grabbed her hands and hugged her until she calmed down.

"Look at me." She kept shaking her head.

"Isa, Look at me." I lifted her chin and stared in her eyes.

"I will take the charge before I let you sit another day in jail. Do you understand me? You will never go to jail again."

"Brayden, I."

"I don't want to hear anything else about it. Can we talk about this at a later date? I want to get her home." The lawyer agreed she that needed to relax.

After the lawyer left we followed and I brought her to my moms house to see the kids. They ran to her and Katarina asked a million questions but Abel just held her. My mom asked me what happened so I took her in the kitchen and explained it all. She wasn't happy hearing I offered myself to take the charge but she understood. The guy she's been with over the last few years is the District Attorney and he's the one who called my mom when the prosecutor dropped the file on his desk. She was going to call me but Isa got to me first.

We stayed at my moms' house and Lira rung my phone off the hook the entire time. I told her we needed a break but she didn't comprehend English. I stepped in the living room and Isa was lying on the couch with the kids. Stress was written all over her face. I took Abel from her and laid him in the crib my mom had over here and then went back to Katarina. Isa ended up going in the kitchen and making herself something to eat. She stopped when I came in, which isn't normal because she knows I don't care how much she eats.

"I'm hungry Birch."

"I didn't say anything. You know your eating habits don't bother me." I sat in one of the chairs staring at her. My phone started ringing again. I shut it off and placed it on the table.

"Thanks for coming to get me." She sat the plate down and took a seat.

"I would never allow you to sit there. How long were you there?" She put her head down.

"Three days." She mumbled.

"THREE DAYS ISA." No wonder she was in the county and not at the station.

"I didn't want to call Maylan because she was at her baby shower and you told me never to speak to you again. I only called because deep down, I knew you wouldn't leave me there. I'm sorry for not listening to you when you were looking out for me."

"Isa, I know you wanted to believe he was there for the kids but you were a pawn in his game. Unfortunately, you are now being hit with FED charges. I'm going to do everything I can to make sure they go away."

"Birch, I can't tell on him. He's going to kill me and-"

"Isa, I wouldn't even allow you to snitch. He's going to fall on his own and we'll both be standing there watching." She finished eating her food in silence. Afterwards I made sure the house was locked up and followed her upstairs.

"Brayden if I go to jail please take care of the kids and when this one comes make sure you bring him or her to see me."

"Hold on, you're pregnant." I was shocked but had a big grin on my face. I had been meaning to ask her ever since the guys brought it up but there was always a distraction.

"I think it happened the day at the office when your ex kicked me. We were so careful after the, you know." She didn't want to mention the abortion.

"I stopped by to tell you the day it rained but we ended up having sex. The next morning I planned on telling you but your girlfriend stopped by and." She covered her mouth.

"Birch I'm sorry. I forgot about her and you've been here with me. You want me to walk you out? I'm sure it was her calling you." I closed the bedroom door and locked it.

"I'm exactly where I want to be and with the person I should be with."

I wrapped my arms around her waist from the back and kissed her neck. Her hand was on the back of my head.

"Why did God make me such a weak woman?"

10

"Isa, in other people's eyes you may be considered weak because you're not doing things they would, if they were in your situation. It doesn't make you weak at all. So what, you're not a fighter. So what, you didn't listen and ended up in jail. I'm sure you learned your lesson. Isa look." I turned her around to face me.

"God made everyone different and yes some things should have been common sense but I get it. You've been on your own for a while and wanted to see the good in everyone. As far as fighting, women know who they can fuck with and who they can't. The day Maylan was shot, Lique tried to talk shit to Lira but she shut Lique down. They haven't had a problem since. I'm not saying you have to turn into the bionic woman, because as long as I'm around, I'll always have your back, male or female. However, I do think I should teach you how to fight."

"Birch, I don't like fighting."

"I know and you learning doesn't mean you'll get into one right away or even have one at all. But Isa, women have you at a disadvantage and as long as they do, they'll continue to come for you."

"You think I should go to self defense class?"

"That's up to you but I'm still going to show you myself."

She nodded her head and ran her hand down my face as she stared at me.

"Are you sure about having a baby with me?"

"I've been squirting in that good ass pussy for a reason."

"Birch you didn't."

"What? It is good and I told you, I was putting a baby in you." I cupped her face with both hands.

"One day you'll be my wife Isa. We are going to have a house full of kids."

I kissed her and she backed away to remove her pajamas. My man stood straight up when he saw her naked.

"I love you Isa Harrison."

"I love you too Brayden Glover."

"From here on out you're mine and there's no breaking up." I told her and she nodded her head.

"My mom is going to be excited. She's wanted me to knock you up for a while now."

"She knows."

"Huh?"

"You do know your mom and I are tight."

11

"Yea but."

"Don't even think about getting mad. Just know she's been waiting for me to tell you so she could tell everyone. Now come let your woman do that special thing you like."

Soon as she said that my attitude vanished. My woman definitely satisfied the hell out of me all night.

Vernon

I got to the house and saw how distraught Maylan looked and then to my left noticed Celeste. In my mind my ex did something and if that's the case all hell is going to break loose. I helped my girl to the car and sped to the hospital, praying both her and my kid were ok. She squeezed my hand so tight; I now understood what men said about women having super strength during labor. I parked in front of the emergency department and her water broke as she stepped out. I waved for the reception lady to come help and she ran back in and came with two nurses pushing a wheelchair.

Maylan sat down and wouldn't let go of my hand. I went in the room and watched them help her get undressed and hook her up to all these monitors. I knew a little of what was about to take place from Maylan making me watch those damn TLC baby shows. Birch and everyone came up just as the anesthesiologist took out some big ass needle to put in her back to numb the pain. That was my cue to stand outside. The doctor called me just as I heard Birch yell to *"Isa what are you doing in jail"*? I told him to handle that and come up later.

"Push baby. I see the head." My mom yelled out. Yea, I stayed at the other end of the bed wiping her forehead and coaching her. If I saw her pussy open up that wide, it may be a chance I stop fucking with her. Say what you want but a human is coming out and with all that blood and shit; I'm good over here.

"Vernon it hurts." She cried looking up at me. I hated to see her in pain.

"I thought the medication was supposed to help."

"It does a little but I still feel pressure and my head is hurting and so is my back." I kissed her lips.

"A few more pushes baby and it's all over." She nodded her head and pushed when the doctor said.

"Congratulations, it's a boy."

"YES!" I shouted and May rolled her eyes.

"I knew it." The doctor let me cut the umbilical cord when he laid him on her chest. The nurse picked him up and took him to the other side of the room to clean and take his foot and hand prints. She handed him back to me as the doctor pushed some nasty shit out of May and stitched her up. He said my son was so big; he tore her up down there. She won't feel it right now but when the medication

13

wears off she will.

"I love you Maylan and I think it's time."

"I love you too Vernon but what are you talking about?" Dawn and everyone else walked in. I wanted Birch up here but I know he was dealing with a lot.

"Oh my God Vernon." She covered her mouth. I took the ring out and sat next to her on the bed.

"Maylan, I don't really know what to say when it comes to proposing, but know you're the only woman who has come in my life and made me change for the better. I know we went through a lot to get here but there's no one else I love more than you and my son. I love the fuck out of you woman and I want to know if you'll marry me?" My mom took the baby from her. She sat up slowly and pulled my face to hers.

"Vernon you are everything I want in a man. You messed up big time and you still have a lot of making up to do. If you can promise never to hurt me again, I'll marry you today."

"I promise I won't May." I slid the ring on her finger and my hand went behind her neck. I pulled her face closer to me and kissed her passionately. If we could have sex right now, we would.

"You can come in now." I heard my mom say and in walked the reverend. I watched Maylan's face go into shock.

"Vernon what's this?" Dawn walked over and placed a veil on her head.

"You said you'll marry me today and that's exactly what's about to happen."

"But what if I said no." She asked fixing the veil and complaining that it didn't match the hospital gown.

"This dick too good for you to say no." I heard her suck her teeth.

"Vernon I look like shit." She snatched the veil off.

"You're beautiful to me May and you just delivered my son. We're getting married so let Dawn put some lip-gloss on your lips or something.

She let Dawn make her presentable and the reverend performed a quick ceremony. I didn't want to stop kissing her and everyone must've known because they stepped out to give us privacy. Maylan had me stand in front of her and pleased me so good with her mouth; I literally bit my lip holding in my moan. The head was so good I could definitely hold out if she did me like that until the six weeks is

14

up.

"That's exactly why you're the wife." I kissed her and helped her to the bathroom. She wanted to wash up a little and clean her mouth before they brought my son back in.

"I thought you loved me for me."

"Oh, I'm in love with you but I'm in love with that pussy and what your mouth can do too." I laughed when she smacked me on the arm.

I made sure she was covered up before I opened the door. Dawn came in and sat in the chair next to her, who asked me to go get my son out the nursery. I left them in the room and walked to get him. I thought my mind was playing tricks on me when I saw Celeste standing at the window. My girl would have a fit if she knew this bitch were here. I grabbed her by the hair and swung her in front of me.

"Bitch are you crazy?"

"I'm sorry Vernon. I just wanted to see if he was yours." She cried trying to move my hands.

"I told you before he was mine."

"I know but you said she was cheating."

"Celeste, one... I don't owe you an explanation on shit about what I do with my girl. And two.... I'm about to get a test done."

"Vernon I-" I tossed her to the side when I saw Maylan in the wheelchair being pushed by my mom with tears coming down her face. She asked me to come get my son so why was she in the hallway anyway?

"You don't think he's yours Vernon?" I walked over to her.

"I didn't say that May but I'm not going to lie; in my heart I feel he's mine but in my head, I'm not sure. We were separated and." She shook her head.

"I want you to get the test done and I would like for you to leave."

"Leave Maylan. I'm not going anywhere."

"Oh but you are."

"Were married now May so you're stuck."

"Married!" Celeste shouted.

"No were not. You forgot the reverend handed me the papers back because in order for it to be legal, I had to sign on the dotted line since you got them without me. I'm not even sure how you did it nor do I care. You can have this ring, the marriage and that bitch." She tore the papers up and all I saw was red. I lifted her up out the chair and

15

stared in her eyes, and all I saw was hate.

"Vernon put her down. She just gave birth and you have her hemmed up. What the fuck is wrong with you?" I heard my mom yelling and trying to pry my hands off her.

"Maylan, I suggest you get ready to sign those fucking papers because if you don't, I'll make sure you never see my son again." I started walking off.

"Oh, he's your son now? Fuck you Vernon and stay the hell away from me. I hate you so much and I wish we never met." I ran down on her.

"You hate me Maylan? I buy you a house, a car, I give you a baby and I picked you as my wife but you hate me."

"Just go Vernon. I didn't ask you for any of the shit you gave. You can have it all except my son. We will co-parent and that's it. Every time I turn around this bitch is around. It's obvious the two of you belong together."

"I don't want her May." I lifted her face to look at me.

"Why is she here Vernon? Huh? I don't even care about the DNA test honestly, I was going to ask you to get it, to ease any doubt you may have but the fact that you told this chick is a problem. What we go through doesn't concern her but here she is and you're telling her your plans. I would never give my ex as much information that you've given her."

"Maylan, she was here when I came to get him."

"Exactly! She felt comfortable to come here to support you regardless of everything. Thanks Celeste for showing me the two of you belong together. Oh and you hitting me with the two by four a while back didn't make me leave him alone but it should've."

"What?"

"No need to get mad now Vernon. You had an idea about it and did nothing. I will always love you but this is what's best right now. Can you take me back to the room please?" She asked my mom who rolled her eyes.

"Maylan we'll never be over."

"FUCK YOU VERNON. I DONT WANT TO SEE YOU AGAIN." She stuck her middle finger up and never turned around.

"Vernon, I didn't mean to cause." Celeste said pretending to feel bad.

"Yes you did. You knew exactly what you were doing. You may not have expected to see her but you did know."

16

"I..."

"Shut the fuck up Celeste. You will never, ever come before my wife. Why can't you get that through your head?" I pressed the elevator button.

"You're not married."

"That paper doesn't mean shit to me. Maylan has always been my wife and paper or not, she still is." I glanced down at the ring she threw at me and stepped on the elevator. Celeste tried to get on with me but I pushed her back.

"If you go anywhere near her or my son, I will fucking kill you." I said it with so much authority she covered her mouth. She knew I wasn't playing and Maylan is going to learn too, that when I said we would never be over, I meant it.

Maylan

Why do I keep taking him back? What is it about him that makes me need him? I asked myself these questions and so many others in my head. My son was asleep on my chest when I felt him being lifted. I didn't bother looking because the only other person allowed here this late is his father. I laid there wiping my tears that continued to fall. I stared at Vernon feed our son and wanted so bad to kiss him but I can't keep living like this. Something's got to give or I'm going to really end up hating him. I know I told him I did but in the heat of the moment, a person will say anything.

I heard him burping my son and took this time to go shower. We were going home tomorrow and I wanted to make sure once I showered there weren't any problems. My body was definitely sore and in pain but being dirty wasn't an option. I picked up the sponge Vernon's mom brought me and squirted the pear body wash on it and lathered up; being extra careful around my vagina. Once I was clean, washed my hair, dried off and put on the pajamas, I got in the bed and turned on my side not facing him. VJ who we made a junior was knocked out in his crib. Vernon had his head back as he slouched down in the chair.

"I'm sorry Maylan." He said scooting me over to lie down with me. He pulled me close and rested his head on mine.

"Vernon, I'm done fighting for a man who doesn't know what he wants."

"Maylan, I only want you. You were right by saying I made her comfortable in thinking she could support me. I should've never said anything to her about our son. I swear on everything that you are the only woman I want. Baby I need you in my life; now more than ever." I wiped my eyes and turned on my back to stare at him.

"Why do you need me Vernon?" He kissed my forehead.

"For one you're the only one who fucks the shit out of me." I rolled back on my side.

"It's true but I need you for more than sex. May you stimulate my mind and that's on some real shit. You calm me down when I'm so upset and all I want to do is murder someone. You listen when I talk and never once have you judged me. When I say I need you it's not bullshit, I really need you. I swear I'll try harder to be the perfect man for you, just don't leave me." By the time he finished, I was hysterical

18

crying. I've never heard a man say he needed me. I could see how watery his eyes were getting by watching me cry.

"Maylan please say you won't leave."

"Vernon there's so much wrong and I'm not sure you can fix it."

"Just tell me and I will."

"That's the problem right there. I've told you a few times what needed to be done but somehow you end up back with her or other women. You'd rather discuss our issues with someone else, than me. I know you still had doubts about our son and to be honest I wasn't angry. I could see how you assumed another man was in the picture after the text and I would've assumed the same, had the roles been reversed. But that's our son, our business and you we're just as comfortable speaking with her about it, as she is talking about things with you. Hell, she showed up to a house you had built for me with no regards to how I felt. You had her at the hospital when I was shot. She doesn't respect me or us and you don't make her." He was about to speak.

"Yea you probably threaten her but it means nothing when you go right back to her. How do you expect her to respect what we share, when you don't? Vernon there's no doubt in my mind that you love me but you're confused right now. There's a lot going on with us, your friends, the guy trying to kill you and whatever it is with her."

"Fuck her Maylan. It's about us and always will be." He stood up and stared out the window. I got up and went over to him.

"It can never be about us until you're over her. I'm in love with you Vernon and I want you in my life forever but that'll never happen with her around. I'm not saying you want to be with her but you're keeping her around for a reason and it's not just to catch the guy. The two of you have time in and whether you want to admit it or not, you still love her." He didn't respond.

"You and I have a son together which connects us for life. We can co-parent but please, I'm begging you to never have her around the baby. She can disguise her hatred of kids around you all she wants but I know she hates kids."

"Maylan I'm not letting you go."

"Goodbye Vernon." I stood on my tippy toes the best I could and pecked his lips. I climbed back in the bed and cried myself to sleep. I'm not sure what time he left but he wasn't here when my son woke up for his feeding.

19

"Are you ready? And where's your wedding ring? I thought you got married." Isa fired off question after question. This is our first time seeing one another since the day Vernon went to her house and she snapped on him.

"It's over Isa and right now I don't want to talk about it because all I do is cry." She nodded her head, picked up the bag and pushed my son in his stroller.

I went back to my parents' house to stay. I know he built a house for us but it didn't feel right living there without us being a family.

Isa drove me home and Dawn, her kids, Birch and Vernon's mom were waiting for me. They all yelled out surprise and Asha who is Dawn's daughter walked over with a small carvel cake that read congratulations, it's a boy. I appreciated all the love and at this moment, I wished Vernon were here but he has unfinished business to tend to. I'm tired of arguing and fighting with his ex and he should be tired of it too.

****

Over the next few weeks, VJ and I were having the time of our lives. He of course is spoiled as hell and starting to come into his looks. Unfortunately, he is a spitting image of his father and only has my hair. The results came in and I know he got them but I screen shot the paper to him just in case. I never got a response but his mom told me he refused to open the mail. He claimed he knew my son was his, but did he?

My stomach had gone down and my son and I were going out on his first outing. We were only going to the mall but it's better than being stuck in the house, which gets boring.

"Thank you for sending him home to me." I heard her voice behind me. I turned the video on my phone to record this bullshit. I could've called Vernon but for what? I sat the phone down in the stroller, I don't care that it won't capture her face; her voice was good enough.

"What do you want Celeste? I'm sure it's nothing." She tried to lift the top of my sons' stroller. I don't know why she was peeking. I dropped my son off to Vernon's mom house every other day. I know he has photos on his phone and I'm sure she went through it, if they're together. I moved her hand away.

"Fine. I don't need to see his ugly ass anyway."

"Why would you say my son is ugly Celeste?"

"Because his mother is and if you don't want me to see him, he must be as ugly as you." I had to laugh at her.

"But anyway as I was saying. Thank you for leaving him alone. Now we can live in peace and deal with the death of our child." It was like the wind was knocked out of me when she spoke those words.

"Excuse me."

"You heard me right. The day I came to the house and you were in labor I was there to show him my paper from the emergency department stating I had a miscarriage."

"I'm sorry to hear that Celeste. I wouldn't wish that kind of loss on anyone." She rolled her eyes. Here I am being sincere and she's still a bitch.

"Yea well, he was so wrapped up in you; he forgot about me. Now that you no longer want him, I can have him all to myself again." Why she thought he wanted her is beyond me.

"Celeste, I'm not sure why you stopped me but if you'll excuse us we have to go."

"Stay away from Vernon or the next time I shoot you, it won't be in the shoulder." She smirked.

"You shot me."

"Sure did and I'll do it again if you don't leave him alone." She walked off and left me standing there with my mouth wide open. I looked around and found a bench to sit on. I listened to her admit to almost killing me and began to cry. People kept asking if I was ok, including Lique who came out of nowhere.

"I'm fine thank you." She stood there.

"Are you sure? Your son is crying and you act like you can't hear him."

"No, I hear him but I'm trying to get him out the spoiled stage. I guess I should work on that at home." I told her and took him out. I had to think of something so she doesn't tell Birch who will definitely tell Vernon and I don't need that.

"Oh my God. He is so handsome and I hate to tell you this but he looks just like Vernon." I started laughing as I took his bottle out the bag and began feeding him.

"Thanks and I know."

"Look, I know we won't ever be friends but just know I never agreed with how Celeste acted towards you. Yes, I did some foul shit to your friend because I was jealous but eventually got over it. You

21

went to Celeste as a woman and she still remained petty. I'll give it to you though. For a chick that can't fight you stay defending yourself. I can respect that."

"Thank you I guess."

"Between me and you Vernon hasn't wanted Celeste for a while now. Honestly I was happy he found you. You calmed him down a lot when it came to his attitude and I never heard about him cheating on you. When Celeste told me he came back to her the last time, she said you cheated on him first. I told her he was just using her to get back at you but you can't tell her shit."

"Can I ask you something?" I put the blanket on my shoulder to burp VJ.

"What's up?" She asked texting on her phone.

"What type of hold does she have on him?"

"She doesn't. He loves Celeste don't get me wrong but she could never get him the way you did, no matter how hard she tried. He cheated on her so much, one would've thought he was never in a relationship but you changed all that and she hated you for it. He blocked her from calling him, if he saw her out he wouldn't speak and you saw what he did to her when she spit on you. Girl whatever voodoo you and your friend got going on let me in on the secret. I swear him and Birch were the dogs of all dogs but somehow the two of you made an impact to slow them down."

"Well they're back together again." She busted out laughing.

"Who told you that?" When I told her Celeste she sucked her teeth.

"You need to get out more boo. Vernon has been staying with his mom for the last couple of weeks. He only comes out to handle business or go out with the guys. Celeste told you that because she's been trying to get him to at least talk to her but he won't, and you know she's not welcomed at his moms. You can't believe everything she says. Listen I have to go but maybe one day we'll talk over lunch." I nodded my head knowing it won't ever happen. I watched her walk off and took my son in the bathroom to change him. Vernon may not be with her like she says but he still has a lot of issues to handle with her.

Isa

Boom, boom, boom. I heard on the front door. I came home from work early hoping to catch a nap before the kids returned from the baby shower. I wanted to go but me and Vernon aren't on good terms; not that we ever were but after the falling out, its best to stay away. If it were at a center or something I would've gone. Of course, I knew Birch would be there and although I didn't want to see him, it was time to tell him about my pregnancy. I knew he was dropping the kids off and that's when I planned on mentioning it.

Boom, boom, boom. Open up police." Police! I thought to myself and ran down the steps thinking something happened to the kids. I opened the door and was tackled to the ground with a gun put to my head. One of the officers picked me up after handcuffing me and sat me in a patrol car. I watched them go in and out my apartment with bags of items. Thank goodness it was at night and I lived around mostly old people. Shit, it was only six and dark as hell out due to the time change, which right now I appreciated. After an hour of sitting in the car, an officer finally got in and took me down to the station where I was booked. I got no phone call and was shipped off to a county jail. I felt like the officers were making fun of me during the strip search when in fact there was one woman doing it and she wasn't skinny at all.

She tossed me a uniform, some underwear that looked worn so I refused to put them on, a pair of socks and some weird looking shoes. I've been homeless so the attire didn't bother me but the conditions inside the jail did. I've slept better on a bunch of comforters than I did on the piece of mattress they called a bed. The food made me want to vomit but I had to eat for my baby. It took me three days to call Birch because I thought he didn't want to talk to me. I only left my cell when it was time to eat and shower. I jumped up out of my sleep and looked over at Birch who was staring at me.

"It's ok Isa. You're not going back."

"How did you know what I was dreaming about?" I asked as he rubbed my stomach waiting for the baby to kick. I was only three months but he said the kicking could start anytime and he wanted to be the first to feel it.

"You kept yelling; *I can't go to jail.*" I turned to look at him.

"I would never ask you to take the charge for me and if I have

23

to do time just promise me, you won't let him get the kids."

"I'm not promising shit, because you're not doing a day behind bars, ever again. Now take your ass to sleep before I slide up in there."

"Who said I didn't want you too?" He laughed and took over my body until I couldn't cum anymore. He pulled me closer to him and hugged me from behind. I wanted to believe what he said but could I? *Should I?*

****

I picked Maylan up from the hospital a few weeks ago, assuming she would be in great spirits now that she married the love of her life but boy was I wrong. She told me everything that happened and I felt bad for her. She was in love with Vernon but I understood about him needing to close the door to one relationship before trying to open another one. Men thought they could move on fast after breaking up with someone and they may be able too but until they're fully over the woman, they will be drawn together for whatever reasons. I'm glad Lique is no longer a threat as far as Birch but its going to be some shit when the baby comes. I can foresee her giving him problems but that's his shit.

Today Maylan was riding with me to the store to pick some things up for dinner and to spend time alone. Neither of us had our kids and we had a lot to talk about. Vernon was at the house when we dropped VJ off and he looked pitiful as we pulled away but he has the power to change everything. The question is when is he going to do it. We shopped all though the mall courtesy of Birch and Vernon. I had his black card and she was using the money he put in her account every week. We didn't want to but shopping has never hurt anybody. I was in the jewelry store looking at some things when the guy Jared who Maylan used to speak to on the phone, came in.

"Damn, your body went straight back to small after the baby I see." I rolled my eyes listening to his weak ass attempt at Maylan. She smiled and continued looking around with him following her.

"Pick what you want and I'll buy it for you." He said to her as me and the guy discussed a piece I picked out.

"No thank you Jared. But it's very thoughtful of you."

"I know you're single now so let me take you out." She glanced over at me and I turned my head. I refused to be involved with her entertaining another man. She may not be with Vernon but she is playing with fire when it comes to him. He may be a nice guy but the fact he deals with Abel isn't something to take lightly, especially after what happened with me.

"Jared, I'm not sure that's a good idea. I just had a baby and a relationship is not what I'm looking for."

"I know Maylan. Just let me take you out with no strings attached." I heard him say. I couldn't hear anything else after that because he pulled her out the door. I used my personal credit card to pay for my stuff and let the man bag it up. I stepped out and looked around for Maylan. Jared had her leaning against the wall as he stood in front of her talking.

"What's this about Maylan?" I heard and wanted to leave her standing there. Dante is like Vernon so I know its about to be some shit.

"Hey Dante."

"Don't hey Dante me. You just had a baby and already on the prowl for a new nigga. Does my boy know?"

"Dante, we're no longer together." She tried to walk away but Jared snatched her back.

"Yo homie. Don't put your fucking hands on her." I moved Dawn back who had the kids with her.

"Mannnn, go head with that shit. She said her and your boy aren't together. Move the fuck on."

"Jared, what is wrong with you? Don't talk to him like that and why are you grabbing my arm?"

"I can see this is about to go left. I'll hit you up later for that date." Jared kissed her cheek, looked Dante up and down and stepped off.

"Maylan, I don't give a fuck about you not being with Vernon but you're standing here with a motherfucker who works with the same nigga who got your girl thrown in jail and snatching you up already."

"Jail. Isa when did you go to jail?" I forgot with everything going on to even mention the situation to her.

"I'll tell you about it later."

You may not see it but he is trying to get at you for a reason."

"I doubt that. He only asked me out an nothing else."

"Yea ok. You think you're tough I see." He folded his arms.

"I never had a problem with you but you are about to get your ass in some shit you can't get out of." He looked at Dawn.

"I don't want you anywhere around her. When shit hits the fan, and it will, I can't have you or my kids involved in it."

"Oh you're telling her what to do?" Maylan said folding her arms in front of her chest. This entire situation was de ja vu all over again. Dawn took the kids over to where the lounge area was and had them sit there.

"Nah, my woman knows what it is. Don't stand here trying to use that reverse psychology on her. You see she's not a selfish bitch like you."

"Bitch." I had to step in the middle because he was in her face.

"Yea, a selfish one too. Any woman who can raise her kid in the same projects and house for that matter, where her parents tried to sell her for years, is selfish. You had a man buy you everything you needed and you still chose to bring your son to one of the most dangerous hoods out there; all because you were in your feelings over his ex."

"Fuck you Dante. I'm not selfish because I don't want to live there."

"Oh you can't live in the house he bought but you're out here spending his money."

"I have his son."

"I don't see a baby bag anywhere in all this shit you brought so go head with that."

"Dante lets go." Dawn said.

"Listen closely Maylan. I introduced you to my woman because I thought you would be great friends and yes, you had her back when I cheated and I appreciate it. However, she doesn't need a friend who can't grow the fuck up and be a woman about her shit. You running around here mad at the world over something you started." Maylan looked at him.

"Exactly! Had you told Vernon from the beginning about the pregnancy, none of this would be happening. The sneaky texts to another nigga and not mentioning it; that was foul as hell. Then you want to be mad over the petty shit with Celeste. At least when the shit hit the fan with me and Dawn, we worked it out like adults and didn't allow an outsider to break us up. You however are out here thotting it up in my eyes, in hopes to get Vernon mad but we know shit isn't going to work out in your favor. You and I both know my boy will hit you back harder with some shit that will have you ready to commit suicide so don't do it to yourself. Dante was pissed and Maylan looked like she as about to cry.

"You are a weak woman and I don't know what he ever saw in

you." He grabbed Dawn's hand and was about to walk away with her and the kids but turned around.

"Isa, you know I have mad love for you but for future reference, when you see me this angry don't stand in front or anywhere around me. I would never intentionally hurt you but I can't control myself when I get to that point. I'll see you at the dinner tomorrow and make sure I see some of your collard greens and yams on the table." He kissed my cheek and they all left.

I didn't know what to say and walked out the mall with Maylan behind me. I asked her if she wanted me to drop her off at home but she said no and asked me to take her to mine. When we got there Birch was still at work and the kids were at school. I went upstairs to take a short nap but ended up sleeping for two hours. I got up around five and the kids were already home and Birch was in the kitchen cooking fried chicken and some other stuff. I could hear him on the phone with I guess Dante because his responses matched what went down at the mall.

"Mmmmm this chicken taste good." I said chewing on a piece I picked up.

"Let me call you back Dante. My greedy ass girl in here eating before the food is even done." He laughed, hung up and pulled me close.

"Shit hit the fan at the mall huh?" I nodded my head and continued tearing the chicken up.

"Is Maylan still here?"

"Nah, she left when I got here."

"Ok. Anyway thanks for cooking babe." I kissed his lips and went to sit with the kids in the living room but he pulled me back.

"What's with this dinner tomorrow night and why is it at my mom's house?"

"I don't know baby. Your mom wanted everyone to come over and she asked me to help her cook." I smirked. I didn't want to ruin the surprise but his stare started making me feel uneasy.

"Yea ok. It better not be on some the baby ain't mine shit." I busted out laughing at how he said it and how mad he got over it.

"Birch, no man has entered my body since you and I been together. Yes, I slept with my ex to get money to help with the food and bills when I thought Maylan wasn't coming back but after you showed me those photos of him being with another woman; its only been you."

"What about when?"

"Baby, it's only been you. I swear on a stack of bibles Brayden that I haven't been with anyone." I wrapped my arms around his neck.

"I believe you baby. I do suggest you get from in front of me before I bend you over and have grease popping on that ass while I'm hitting it." I couldn't do anything but laugh. He was becoming aroused and I damn sure didn't want the grease hitting me. I walked out and joined the kids. I kept stealing glances at him. Each day it felt like I was falling even deeper in love with him. I pray he's the man for me and no one will take him away.

Birch

"You have a miss Lira here to see you sir." My secretary spoke over the intercom while I was on the phone with my mom.

"Brayden don't get caught up in no shit with her. If you hurt Isa, me and you are going to fight."

"Calm down ma. I invited her here. I have been avoiding her and the best place to speak with her, is in my office."

"Yea ok. I'll see you tonight." My mom said and hung up.

I walked to the door, opened it and gestured for Lira to step in. I can't lie, Lira was working the hell out of the tight ass dress she wore but it wasn't enough to make me mess up what I had with Isa. I pointed to the seat for her to sit but instead she sat on my lap in a straddling position, at the same time Isa walked in. I knew she was coming to take me to lunch and I'm sure this looked suspect. Isa didn't say a word and came over to where we were. I tried to move Lira off my lap but she wouldn't. Lira had no idea Isa was even in the room.

WHAP! Isa smacked the shit out of Lira, shocking the hell out of me.

"Bitch I'm about to." I knocked Lira on the floor and stood over here.

"You ain't about to do shit. I called you here to ask you to stop calling and texting me and you're trying to fuck. She has every right to be upset with you over her man."

"Her man. You weren't her man a few weeks ago when your dick was down my throat and swimming in my pussy." I saw Isa's face turn up.

"Exactly a few weeks ago. She and I weren't together then, so you disclosing that information means nothing."

"Birch I..." I put my hand up.

"I don't want to hear anything you have to say. My woman is ready to take her man to lunch and you're interrupting."

"You asked me here."

"I did and I said what I needed to." She stormed out of the office.

"I guess I got here in time." Isa said sitting in my chair.

"You know I don't want her."

"Yea ok. Anyway I'm hungry." She headed to the door and I pulled her back and made her stand in front of me.

"Don't make me fuck you up Isa. No other woman can do me like you."

"Ssssss Brayden stop." I had my hands circling her pearl in her pants that woke up the second I touched her. Anytime she caught and attitude, this is all I had to do to knock it out of her.

"Nah Isa. I think daddy needs to teach you a lesson." I unbuttoned my pants and tossed Isa over my desk.

"Ahhhhhh, she screamed out as I entered her.

"Stop that screaming and fuck daddy back." I smacked her ass and her cream coated my dick.

"Get off me Brayden." She pushed me back with her ass and turned around smirking.

"You want this pussy?"

"You know I do."

"Then fucking act like it and take it. I mean unless you don't want it anymore." She sat up on my desk with her legs cocked open playing with herself. She has become so comfortable with her body and a nigga loved it.

"Do you want this dick?" I let the tip play around her clit.

"No. I need that dick. Brayden pleaseeeee give it to me."

"I don't think you really want it." Her body was inching under me to try and force me inside. I would back up, as she got closer.

"Fine. I guess I'll get dressed. She turned over on her knees and her ass was in the air. She was being smart. I could see the juices leaving her body as she let her fingers run up and down her folds. I almost came as I stood there watching her.

"Mmmmm girl you taste good." I had my face buried in her pussy and ass.

"Oh Godddddddddd Brayden." I know my secretary had to be bright red hearing Isa because she was loud as hell. I hit the intercom and told my secretary she was done for the day and I'll still pay her. I stopped until I heard the outside door shut.

"Get down." I was nervous she would fall so I made her lean over the couch and entered her forcefully.

"Ahhh shit Isa. This pussy is so fucking good. Ummmm. I'm about to cum already." Her walls were squeezing me and she was so wet I couldn't hold out like I wanted.

"Cum in my mouth baby." She turned around.

"Shitttttttt." I grabbed her head as she sucked every kid out.

"This pussy is going to kill me." She stood up grinning.

"Brayden, I love sucking your dick. You taste so good." She stuck her tongue in my mouth.

"Mmmmm. I think it's time for your woman to fuck you." My man woke right up.

"I love it when you talk dirty." I kissed her as she slid down.

"You do huh?"

"Absolutely. Ride daddy's dick baby." I smacked her ass and she smiled.

"Yea Isa. Do your thing. Ahhh damn." For the next hour we went back and forth in my office pleasing the hell out of one another. Thank goodness I sent my secretary home because both of us were moaning loud as hell with no care in the world.

"I think I'm done for the day." Isa said after we finished. Both of us were breathing fast and lying on the floor in my office.

"Whatever. Let's go eat. You definitely made me work up an appetite." I stood up and helped her to stand. We went in the bathroom and cleaned ourselves up and headed to a late lunch.

****

"Well don't you look cute?" I said to Katarina who came down the steps wearing a red and black dress that flared out at the bottom.

"I know." She grinned. My mom wanted everyone to come dressed up for some reason. Abel came down behind her wearing some black pants with a white dress shirt and some fresh white Jordan's.

"My man." I lifted him up and checked out his fresh hairdo. Dante took him with his stepson to get a haircut earlier. Isa didn't allow anyone to do Katarina's hair except her, Maylan or my mom.

"Damn baby. I think we should cancel the dinner." I put Abel down and met Isa at the bottom of the steps. She wore a dark blue, mid length dress, which had her cleavage showing a little too much, if you ask much me. She had silver strap up shoes on with silver accessories to match. Her hair was laid down and parted in the middle and she had on little makeup. She looked beautiful and I dare someone to say different.

"Thanks baby. Let's go before your mom calls yelling." I pecked her lips and stared as she walked to the door.

"I can't wait to get you back home later." I closed her door and ran on the other side to get in. We drove to my moms' house and I kept stealing glances at Isa when we were at a light. I parked in the driveway and it seemed as if everyone was there. When we walked in

31

they stared at Isa the same way I did and smiled.

"Look at you Isa. You're stunning." My moms boyfriend told her and she blushed. She went in the kitchen where the women were. I sat around with my boys talking about the game when my mom said it was time to eat.

"Where's Maylan?" I looked around and asked Vernon where she was and he shrugged his shoulders. I went to tell Isa but couldn't find her. My mom pointed to the bathroom and had everybody assisting her with setting the table.

"What's wrong baby?"

"Maylan's not coming." She wiped her eyes.

"It's ok Isa."

"No it's not Birch. I wanted her here and she won't come because Dante cursed her out and Vernon is here. I don't understand why she can't be there for me like I am for her." I'm not sure why she's so upset over this damn dinner and Maylan not coming.

"We'll talk about it later. Let's get through this dinner so I can take you home and make you feel better." She shook her head.

By the time we came out the bathroom everyone was seated at the table. My mom had Isa sit next to her and me next to Isa. There was so much food and everyone was here enjoying themselves. My mom stood up making a toast to all of us guys for not failing victim to the streets and becoming men. Once she finished she nodded her head to Isa.

I noticed all our moms smiling and Dawn looked like she was about to cry. Vernon had his chin resting on his knuckles and all the other guys had smirks on their face. I guess I'm the only one who had no idea what the hell was going on. Isa turned her chair to me.

"Brayden, you know I love you right?" I saw her hands shaking and her eyes were glossy.

"What's wrong?" She rubbed her hands on her dress.

"Brayden when we first met I didn't think I had a chance in hell with you." Vernon chuckled. She waved him off.

"The day you drove us to the see the new apartment, I assumed it would be the last time seeing you. When you rescued me and the kids, I knew then, you were the one for me and prayed everyday that you'd want me the way I wanted you." She ran her hands down the side of my face.

"Brayden the joy we share and how we understand each other, is all I could ever ask for in a relationship. I thought love was

32

hard to find until you came in my life. I love everything about you. Your smile is contagious and your touch is so addictive, I can never get enough." I stared at how nervous she was but appreciated the fuck out of what she was doing.

"No one can love me better and I want to be with you until the end of time. I know what we have is real because the way we love each other, makes others envy us." She called the kids over, who Dawn let walk one at a time. Isa got on her knees and I had the biggest grin on my face.

Katarina walked over with a cupcake that had a piece of paper on it stuck to a toothpick. *Will.* Is all that was written on it. Kristopher and Asha came with a cupcake of their own. I opened the paper from them and it said *You* and *Marry*. My son came with the last cupcake that said *Me*. Abel was the last to come and handed me a small box. I opened it and there was a platinum wedding band. I looked up at her as she covered my hand to stop me from taking it out.

"Brayden, I know this isn't the traditional way as far as a proposal but I wanted you to know how much I loved you. If you don't want to wear it right now, I'm ok with that." I didn't say anything.

"Now that the hard part is over. Will you marry me Brayden Glover?" I looked around the room and everyone had grins on their face. I put my head down and ran my hand down my face.

"I can't Isa." She lifted herself from the ground and backed up with a hurt expression.

"Isa." I grabbed her hand and she snatched it back.

"It's ok Brayden. I already knew I wasn't the woman you wanted to marry. I figured, I'd try my luck anyway." I laughed because she always made assumptions. She lifted her glass of water to her lips.

"Isa, I can't accept your proposal not because I don't want to marry you but because you were supposed to wait for me to ask you." I got down on my knee and took the seven-carat pear shaped ring out my pocket. She dropped the glass that was in her hand and water spilled everywhere.

"Isa, you are every woman to me. You came in my life unexpectedly and turned it upside down. I've never met a woman who could slow me down and make me a one-woman man. I love how you love me, the kids and everyone else without expecting anything in return. Your heart is pure and I want us to grow old together. Will you marry me?" She was hysterical crying shaking her head yes. You heard everyone clapping and my son came over to hug her.

"It's about time." Smitty said and Maria popped him upside the head.

"Let me see the ring." Dawn came over to see it. My mom was ecstatic and so was everyone else. I see now why she was so upset Maylan didn't come. It was a big moment for her even though I asked her too. That's something they'll deal with on their own. Right now I'm not about to let anyone steal our happiness, not Lique or Lira. If anyone assumes they will, it will be hell to pay.

Lique

"So you're telling me, you told Dante you were pregnant and he believed you?" Celeste asked Kacey who sat with us in Red Lobster smirking.

"Sure did. He's so damn stupid because we only had sex once. Well a few times in one night but you know what I mean. The next time he came over I was ready. The holes were poked in the box and I know it went through the wrapper but his dick wouldn't get hard." I was disgusted listening to her discussing ways on trapping Dante. I mean she messed around on him to get with Abel. I guess the saying is true about how you don't miss someone until they're gone.

"Girl you crazy. I can't really say much because I did the same thing with Vernon." My mouth fell open when she said it.

"Celeste you hate kids." Kacey told her and finished eating.

"I know that and so does everyone else but I was willing to give him one just because it meant he would remain in my life. I would've been that pain in the ass baby momma too."

"What you mean would've?" Now I was curious. She went on to tell us how she found out about her pregnancy when Vernon beat her up for spitting on Maylan. I was surprised because she never mentioned it to me. She went by his house to tell him but Maylan was in labor so she gave the paper proving it, to Birch. Then she went on and on about how she went to see the baby in the hospital and Maylan broke up with him because he requested a DNA test. The shit was crazy and I've come to realize now, that Celeste is a fucking stalker for real.

"Are you serious right now Celeste?" she shrugged her shoulders.

"What happened with you and Kenta?"

"Nothing. He's still in the picture. I only been around him because he gives me money but I think he has someone else. We used to be inseparable but now he comes once or twice a week if that."

"Why are you pining away for Vernon then?" Kacey asked and we both stared and waited for her to answer.

"Honestly, Vernon is the man I want because I can't have him. Yes, he is a great provider and his sex is out of this world but he ain't shit. I love the hell out of him though."

"But you knew that." I told her.

35

"In the beginning, I didn't think that. Once he cheated, everything changed and not for the better. It was like nothing I did was good enough for him and now this funny looking bitch comes into his life and he gives her not only a house and car, but a got damn baby. I continued to fuck him; hoping he'll see I'm the one down for him; especially since I've been giving him information to Kenta's whereabouts, but he only wants her. I love Vernon but he'll never see me in the way he sees her and because of it, she'll have to suffer the consequences."

"Bitchhhhhh what you plan on doing?" Kacey asked all enthused by it. I had to listen because Maylan didn't seem like a bad person and if the shit was real bad, I would text Birch. Celeste was taking this shit too far in my opinion.

"Well the dude Jared, that Abel brought around is trying to get with her and so far, so good. They went to the club one night but we ended up fighting them and she went back to Vernon. But now that they're over for good, she's been texting back and forth with him non-stop. Jared is a crazy motherfucker though. I was at his house one day and he had this bog brown envelope on his dresser, so of course I was being nosy."

"Ugh, why were you at his house?"

"Girl bye. I've been sleeping with him since he came to town and I must say, he is working with something." I sucked my teeth because she disgusted me more and more with what she was saying. I had no idea she was in the streets giving up her pussy like that.

"I'll tell you what though. If I don't kill Maylan myself, he sure as hell will." Kacey and I looked at her like she was crazy. This bitch talking about murder now, I mean what the hell is really going on?

"Why would he kill her?"

"Girl, he had newspaper clippings about how he's a sociopath, which means he has no feelings or emotions about what he does to women. He murdered his last girlfriend because evidently she was going to leave him for being abusive. I should've taken a photo of the papers but I was so engrossed in what I was reading, I forgot. Shit, that nigga had a list of other shit he did too."

"Ok, so why is he pressing Maylan?"

"I think he wants her to get pregnant so he can have an offspring. He said some shit like if he gets her, then I'll get Vernon back."

"What are you going to do?" I asked trying to get her to say it.

"Hold on." She stopped mid conversation when she saw Vernon walk in with the baby and his mom. She stood up and luckily for us they were only two seats over and it wasn't crowded so we could hear everything.

"Why are you over here?" His mom said and looked her up and down. You could see Vernon taking the blanket off the baby and lifting him up in his arms.

"Oh shit bitch. The baby looks just like him." I nodded my head and told her I knew already from when I saw Maylan at the mall.

"I came to say congratulations to the new daddy."

"Get the fuck out my face Celeste."

"Vernon why are you treating me like this? You know we'll always be together." He laughed and handed the baby to his mom. I could see how upset he looked and prayed he didn't whoop Celeste ass again. I'm not picking her big ass up off the ground this time.

"Celeste, I'm going to say this one time and I hope you listen and hear me." He stood up and she backed up to where we were.

"I should've known you were with these two idiots." He pointed at us.

"Fuck you." Kacey said.

"No thanks." He said focusing back on Celeste.

"Celeste, I don't want you anymore. Why can't you get that through your fucking head?"

"You weren't saying that a while ago."

"I was using your dumb ass to get information on the married nigga you sleeping with."

"What married man? No one I messed with is married."

"You need to do a better background check on the niggas you fuck. Kenta is married with kids so whatever you thought y'all had will never be."

"What?" You could see Celeste was hurt and shocked.

"Stay the fuck away from me Celeste." He went to walk away and looked over his shoulder. She stood there still in shock by what he revealed.

"Oh, and if you ever call my son ugly again, I'm going to beat your ass worse than the last time."

"I didn't call your baby ugly."

"The one thing I can say about Maylan is she has never lied to me. I know you said it because you're jealous of Maylan and what she and I share or shared, but that's over thanks to your hateful ass for

37

breaking us up. She could and still can get whatever she wants from me. I told you that day in the hospital not to fuck with her and that still stands. You may not have laid hands on her but if you say anything to her, it counts as you fucking with her. I suggest you get out your feelings and move on." He mushed her so hard she hit the ground. You heard the waiters and waitresses laughing and his mom had a smile on her face. She used to love Celeste but she didn't approve of the way she went around trying to cause problems.

"You'll never be with her again because the next nigga has had her legs in the air and her ass tooted up for the past few nights." She chuckled and got up off the floor. Vernon had her yanked up.

"What the fuck you say?" Her shirt was balled up in his hands as he stared in her face.

"You're sitting here treating me like shit and claiming her, when the next nigga, digging her back out. Oh yea, he fucking the hell out of her. How did he put it? She got some good pussy and her head is even better." He let her go and she started laughing. I saw him putting his son back in the carrier and we watched them leave in a hurry. I felt sorry for Maylan but Celeste is going to get herself killed if she keeps playing this game with him.

"You know he's about to go find her." Kacey laughed putting her money out to pay for her food.

"Fuck her. Shit, once he finds out, he'll be right in my bed and a bitch is good with that. As far as Kenta, I am about to text him about his little wife."

"Celeste you can't be mad at him when you were back and forth with him and Vernon."

"I know but he still should've told me." She pulled her phone out.

"Oh Lique, did you tell your baby daddy he isn't the father? I mean, now that you got those results back, its only fair to let him know." I gave her a hateful stare. This bitch was coming for me and I didn't appreciate it.

"Wait! That's not Birch's baby?" Kacey asked and looked confused.

"Nope and the guy she pregnant by has a girlfriend, even thought they're not seeing eye to eye now. I think she should mention it to her too. Don't you think Lique?" I slammed my money down and bounced. I see now that Celeste is going to do everything in her power to make sure Kacey is aware. I'm not sure why she's acting like I owe

Kacey an explanation. Yes, we speak but I met her through Celeste. She isn't my friend and when she was supposedly with Dante, I wasn't with Birch yet so we didn't know each other through them either.

I got the results to the DNA Abel and I took and he is 99.99% the father of my baby, which I knew. Once I figured there was a baby in my stomach, I went to the doctors right away and the date of conception was definitely when I was with Abel. Yes, Birch and I had unprotected sex and he came in my mouth and once inside me but Abel and I always had sex raw, so the possibility was always there.

I had no doubt after that but I loved to see the hurt on Isa's face when she found out it was supposedly by Birch. It's like she had kryptonite in her pussy or something by how hard he fell for her. Shit, I was with him for over five years and couldn't get the nigga to commit to anything. Granted I stayed when I should've left but his money and dick kept me there. I know women say that a lot but when you have a man who has money and can dick you down properly you tend to let shit slide.

I got in my car and sent a message to Birch saying I needed to talk to him. She can play all the games she wants but I'm going to have the last laugh. Birch hit me back and said he was at his house and to stop by. At first I wasn't sure it was the right idea but if he told me to come, she must not be there. I parked in his driveway and walked to the door after grabbing all my things out. He opened it in just a wife beater and some sweats. I had to stop myself from drooling. My baby daddy is fine and he still had an affect on me. My son waved and walked by with Isa's little son, well Abel's son behind him.

"Daddy why is she here?" Katarina said and I listened to him answer. I was shocked she called him that and even more, that he answered her.

"What's up Lique?" He didn't invite me in and I was a little pissed about it. Shit, I've been to this house a million times, had sex in it and even stayed here a lot.

"Hello Lique." I saw Isa come up behind him and wrap her arms around his waist. He smiled and pulled her in front of him and kissed her lips.

"I'm about to start the movie." She said.

"I'll be done in a minute. Make sure Brayden doesn't take my spot."

"Oh no. I'm not getting in that again. The last time you stopped speaking to me for an hour because I let him sit by me."

"Whatever."

"It was good seeing you Lique and thanks for not having a problem with Brayden being here. I absolutely love him and so do the kids." She laughed and waved goodbye. I noticed the big ass rock on her finger and started dry heaving. I know damn well this nigga didn't propose to her fat, ugly ass. Yes, I started hating right away.

"Birch, did you ask her to marry you?" He folded his arms across his chest.

"Why would you ask me a question you already know the answer too. I peeped you staring at her ring but since you're on that petty shit. Yes, I did ask her to marry me and she said yes." I felt my eyes getting watery.

"You never asked me."

"Lique you weren't wife material and you know it. Anyway, what did you want to talk to me about?" He asked totally bypassing the fact of how hurt I was.

"Nothing. Never mind."

"Lique you wanted something."

"I did but it doesn't matter." I went to leave.

"I'll be by to get my son tomorrow."

"Yea ok."

"Birch, I can see my son."

"You can but it's been over two weeks and I haven't seen as much as a *hello* or *how is my son* text come through my phone. You haven't even called to speak with him. I can see you're in your feelings over my fiancé's ring but she is going to be around so get used to it." He moved closer to me.

"If you even think about having my son around Abel, I will not only beat your ass but take him from you."

"How are you going to tell me who to have my son around?"

"Because that nigga got my girls house raided and she was arrested." I covered my mouth because Abel never mentioned it to me.

"And if you're wondering what her charges her, I'll give you a few. Kingpin, racketeering, endangering the welfare of a child, weapons charges." I put my hand up.

"Oh you don't want me to finish?" He asked sarcastically.

"Birch I don't think he knew she was there. I can't see him-" he cut me off.

"What you think because you're a bad bitch he won't get you

caught up?" He threw his head back laughing.

"Isa may not be a video vixen but that nigga loved and probably still loves her and he still let those niggas distribute shit from her house. He may not have been there but he was well aware of the transactions being made out her back door. Thank goodness the kids weren't there. I'm going to let you in on a little secret though." He moved his mouth to my ear.

"That nigga is going to fall and you better hope you're nowhere around when he does because I can tell you now, not to use that one phone call to call me." He backed up with a smirk on his face. I turned the key in my ignition and watched him walk back in his house. Did Abel know he was under investigation? Should I be around him? *Fuck!* I drove straight to the house he and I have been staying at and walked in the room to see him getting dressed.

Abel

I've been trying to reach Isa for the last few weeks. I haven't heard from her nor have I seen my kids. Kacey told me she's been staying with Birch but why, when she has her own place and I furnished it with new stuff. It took me a week to get my business up and running out of a new apartment again but its back to the money as usual. I planned on going to Birch's house and bring her ass back home. She can date the nigga all she wants but living with him, yea; I'm not having that. Say what you want but she will always be mine and once I get her to lose weight, she'll be just as bad as the next chick. I love the shit out of Isa but the hurt from the past is still there. I'm trying to make it up to her but she acts like this isn't her address anymore.

I put some clothes on and was headed over to Lique's apartment. She text me and said we had to talk because Celeste was trying to blow her spot up. I told Lique when we first started messing around to mention it to Kacey. Granted, they are more acquaintances than anything but they shouldn't be hanging together either.

Lique can fight her ass off but I think she's more worried about losing the baby and now that I found out the kid is mine, there ain't no way Kacey will lie hands on her. She can be mad at Lique from a distance and even fight her afterwards but during the pregnancy, Kacey can cancel that.

"Abel, tell me you didn't know Isa was in jail." Lique said coming in the room and dropping her things at the door.

"What are you talking about and didn't I say to meet me at your apartment?" I sat on the bed and leaned over to lace up my sneakers.

"Isa went to jail behind a raid in her house." I sat up and stared at her to see if she was playing.

"Fuck. I have to get her out." I started rushing and grabbing my stuff. I had no idea she was caught up because I didn't have anyone to send down there to ask questions.

"Abel, she's fine." I took my hand off the doorknob.

"How do you know?"

"I went by his house to mention the shit Celeste had cooked up in her head about Maylan and she was there. Abel, he proposed to her and she accepted." My entire facial expression changed from worried to pissed the fuck off.

"Who told you that?"

"I saw the ring and he called her his fiancé." She scooted back in the bed and laid there. I think we were both in our feelings over it because neither of us said a word.

"I'll be back." I snatched my keys off the dresser and sped to his house. I parked in his driveway, jumped out and banged on the door. Isa came out looking as beautiful as ever and had a glow around her.

"Abel what are you doing here?"

"Are you marrying that nigga?"

"Yes I am." She said with confidence in her voice.

"Not if I can help it." Her eyes got big.

"Abel, why don't you want me to be happy?"

"What?" I asked and looked around waiting for him to come out.

"He makes me happy and isn't ashamed of me. Abel, he loves the kids and-"

"I don't want to hear that shit. You will always be mine; now call him down here so we can talk." She slammed the door in my face. I stood out there a few minutes thinking she told him I was here but she must not have, so I banged on the door again.

"He's not here Abel." She tried to close the door and I stepped in making her move back.

"Abel, you have to go."

"Why you acting like that Isa?" I leaned in to kiss her.

"Abel, please go. I don't want you anymore."

"That's what your mouth say."

`"You're being real disrespectful coming in his house." I backed her against the wall.

"His house. I thought it was both of yours." She sucked her teeth.

"Nah bro. Her house is being built from the ground up and I'm positive she asked you to leave." I chuckled and turned around to see him standing there with Dante and Smitty.

"Actually she didn't."

"Abel, I did tell you to leave; more than once." Isa told him and rolled her eyes at me.

"It's all good Isa. Where are the kids?"

"Upstairs."

"Do me a favor baby and go join them. I'll be up shortly." He kissed her and she walked up the steps. I watched her ass sway back and forth.

"This nigga." I heard and saw Birch shaking his head.

"Not only did you come in my house and didn't leave when my fiancé asked but you're staring at her ass."

"What can I say? A nigga miss that good ass pussy. Yo, did she learn new tricks with her tongue when she gives head? She was a beast at sucking dick." I smirked and shoulder checked him on the way out.

"My woman's sex game will never be up for a debate. But just so you know; don't bring your ass over here again."

"Maybe. Maybe not."

"What kind of man brings his business to where his kids sleep at night? Huh? Or allows his kids mother to sit in jail for something she knew nothing about? You went through all of the chasing to get Isa back; just to push shit out her house?" He came closer.

"And for the record. I know for a fact you haven't been fucking or getting your dick sucked by her. You can talk that shit you want but we both know what it is."

"If you say so." I knew he was getting mad and kept egging him on.

"I'm trying to remain calm but you're making it hard. I suggest you move on." Birch is far from a punk but I also know he doesn't like to be provoked nor did he want the kids to see.

"Just tell Isa to bring her ass home tonight."

"She is home motherfucker."

"Lets go Birch. He isn't worth it." Smitty said while Dante grilled the hell out of me.

"Oh Birch. I forgot to tell you that Lique's pussy is good too. Thanks for sharing." I thought that would trigger him but he laughed. It only made me think of something else to say.

"Her shit doesn't taste better than Isa's though. Damn, I can still taste her on my tongue." He walked up on me and stole the shit out of my mouth.

"Oh you want to fight." I don't know why my dumb ass asked that question. Birch had his shirt off and hit me again and before I knew it, we were going at it outside his house.

"Birch please stop." I could hear Isa yelling in the background. He looked at her and she was about to cry. I charged at him; knocking him on the ground and somehow he flipped me over and I felt him punching me in my ribs. Not too long after he stood up and began kicking me everywhere.

"Birch, I need to get to the hospital." All movement ceased when she said that.

"What's wrong?" He ran to her.

"Something is wrong with the baby." I looked at her assuming she was speaking of my son, until I saw her holding her stomach. What the fuck? These two are about to have a kid together. Oh hell no. He started walking her to the car and I mustered up all the strength I had to get up.

I made my way to where they were and kicked him so hard in the back, he went flying forward and his head hit the corner of the door and then bounced off the pavement. Isa started screaming and there was blood coming from his head. I noticed Dante coming in my direction and walked fast to my car. Not because I was scared but more or less because I didn't have any fight left in me.

I pulled off just as Dante opened my door. I glanced in my rear view mirror and noticed Dante's car trailing me. I swerved in and out of traffic trying to get away. We stopped at a light and the nigga hit the back of my car so hard, I went off the road and in a ditch. Thank goodness it was a small one and I'm able to walk away but I definitely need to get to the hospital. Those kicks fucked me up and I probably have some cracked ribs.

"Isa he's going to be fine. You have to calm down." His mom said to me holding my hand.

"Ma, you didn't see all the blood." I started calling her that when Birch proposed.

"I know honey but you're stressing out the baby."

"I want to see him." I wiped the tears down my face.

"Isa, the doctors are with him now. They'll update us shortly but in the meantime you have to stay calm. They said you were ok for now but if you continue working yourself up; they'll have to admit you." I laid my head on her shoulder and took deep breaths trying to relax.

Abel made Birch hit his head really hard on the corner of the car door, which dazed him and he fell on the cement, hitting his head harder. He had a gash on the front of his head and when Smitty turned him over, there was a huge one in the back with blood gushing out. The sight alone made me vomit. I dialed 911 and Smitty called Maria to come sit with the kids. He stayed until she got there and I went in the ambulance with him. He kept going in and out of consciousness. I kissed his lips when we got there and they took him right in.

We sat there for over three hours and still hadn't heard a word. Vernon came in not too long ago and you could tell he had something on his mind but he wouldn't dare stay home. I went to sit by him and rubbed his back. Him and Birch were the tightest out the crew so I knew he'd be upset. It was out of the ordinary and I saw everyone looking at me. I shrugged my shoulders and told him Birch is a fighter and he'll be ok. Shit, I had to convince myself of the words I told him. He had a lot of blood loss and you can't fuck around with the head.

"Thanks Isa." He said shocking the hell out of me.

"Ugh ok."

"Look. I know I've been the shitty asshole to you all this time and I apologize."

"Vernon you don't." He cut me off.

"Yea I do. My brother loves the hell out of you and all he wanted was for me to respect you and I couldn't. It's not even a reason why I couldn't; I just didn't. You're not the type of woman I'm used to seeing him with and I felt he could do better." I heard someone suck their teeth.

"I never took the time out to see past your looks and realize how much you love him. I mean he's never been faithful, had a woman live with him or show her off. He's never asked a woman to marry him or had one ask him either but he did all that and more for you. As much as I don't want to admit it, you two are meant for each other. I actually envy y'all relationship and wish me and Maylan had the same." I wiped the few tears that fell. To hear Vernon say all that made me realize he's not such an asshole after all. He was looking out for his brother in his eyes and I can respect that.

"Isa, I swear I won't disrespect you again and I'm sorry for all the times I upset you or even made you cry behind close doors. No woman should be treated the way I treated you, regardless of what she looked like."

"Awwww, my baby growing up." Birch's mom and his mom said. They came to hug him but he put his arm out curving them. Of course they smacked him in the back of the head.

"Are you the family of Brayden Glover?" We all stood up.

"Brayden suffered a really bad concussion and he had to get twenty stitches in the back of his head and five in the front. We ran an MRI and cat scan on him and found he had a little cyst in the back of his head. It's the size of a nickel but nothing we're concerned about. Also, he did suffer a fractured rib; I'm assuming from the fall. He will have headaches for the next week or two. I also want to keep him for a few days to run an EEG and some other tests on him, to make sure no seizure activity is going on. Otherwise, he's going to be fine."

"Can we see him?" I asked.

"Oh yes. We didn't allow anyone back there because we took him in for testing right away and had him heavily medicated. He was just waking up when I came out to speak with you but feel free to see him. He'll be transported to another floor shortly." He shook all of our hands and handed his mom a business card.

"Go head Isa. We can wait." His mom said and they all agreed. I didn't know what to expect and braced myself for the worst. It didn't matter that the doctor said he was ok, seeing him is different.

"Hey baby." I said when I walked in the room. He had the television remote in his hand.

"How's my baby? You didn't lose it, did you? Are you ok?" I smiled listening to him worry about me.

"I'm fine Brayden. How are you feeling?"

"Right now, I'm good but the doctor said I will have a lot of headaches." He moved over a little and lifted the covers for me to lay with him.

"You know I'm too big to fit on the bed with you. Are you sure you want me to get in?"

"Isa don't put yourself down like that. It makes me uncomfortable and you don't need confirmation from me to ever lie in the same bed. You are about to be my wife and I want you to stay the confident and independent woman you have grown into."

"I'm sorry Brayden. It's just whenever I see him, all the memories come up and I start losing myself again. I appreciate you for teaching me to love myself and I'm getting better everyday because of you."

"I know it's hard Isa but your man will always have your back. Remember that. Now get in the bed so I can rub on my pussy and go to sleep." I laughed and took my shoes off to join him. He laid on his side staring at me while his head rested on his arm.

"I'm going to kill him Isa."

I didn't say anything because there's nothing to say. He's going to do what he wants and after Abel did this; I can't blame him. I snuggled under him and felt his other arm on my side. Thank goodness he forgot about playing with my pussy because we'd be in here having sex by now. He kissed my forehead and I heard the buttons to the remote clicking. I'm not sure how long I was asleep but when I woke up Birch was asleep next to me and Vernon, Smitty and Barry were laid up in some chairs knocked out. Dante was most likely with Dawn since she's almost due. He refused to leave her alone for too long.

I got up to use the bathroom and when I came out Maylan was standing there. She didn't see me but I watched as she walked over to Vernon and stared as he slept. It's been a couple of weeks since I've seen her. The two of them belonged together but they're both stubborn. She bent down and kissed his cheek. I got in the bed with Birch and pretended she wasn't there. I heard her calling my name but why should I respond? When I needed her she refused to be there for me. Granted, I missed the baby shower but a bitch was in jail. I would never do her the way she did me.

"Baby, Maylan is here." I heard Birch say but didn't look at him.

"Tell her to leave." I kept my eyes on the television. I could tell he didn't know what to say.

"Isa please talk to me."

"No. Now get the fuck out of here." By now Vernon, Smitty and Barry had woken up.

"What the fuck happened to you Maylan?" Vernon jumped up and ran to her. I turned to look at why he said that. She had a black eye, red marks around her neck and two splints on her fingers. I didn't notice it because it was dark in the room with the exception of the TV.

"I'm fine Vernon."

"You are not fine. Who did this to you?" She stood there crying and when I didn't get up she ran out the room.

"Isa why didn't you?" I cut Birch off.

"Because I'm tired of being there for everyone and no one is there for me. Ever since we left the shed, I've been the backbone and it's time for me to watch out for myself. I needed her to be there when I had the abortion but she was mad over something with her parents. I needed her when your ex and his ex put me and Katarina in the hospital but she chose Vernon over us." I could tell they all felt bad listening to me.

"I'm not blaming anyone because those are her choices. Then I needed her when I proposed to you and she refused to come because Dante put her in her place. Each time I wanted my best friend, my sister around me for important things she bailed. I'm trying to be strong for everybody but I can only take so much." I covered my face up with the blanket and cried.

"I'll see y'all tomorrow." I heard Birch saying.

"Isa." Vernon called my name and I took the covers off my face.

"I'm sorry if you felt like she chose me over you. I know how close you two are but don't let her burdens get you down. I got Maylan so don't worry about it. I know it's easier said than done but she is my sons mother and I'm going to always make sure she's good." He kissed my cheek and Birch tried to punch him in the chest.

"What's that about?"

I told him how Vernon apologized and all the nice things he said. Birch was surprised but I could see the small smile on his face. I think it put him at ease too. The nurse came in not too long after and they transported him to a new room. Luckily he didn't have a roommate because I damn sure took a shower and changed into the clothes his mom brought up when she came.

"Birch are you ok? Oh my God." I heard a woman say as I slid on my leggings. I opened the door and Lira stood there barely dressed. It looks like she was about to go out or she came here on purpose in that attire.

"First off, my girl is in the bathroom and second how did you even know I was here?"

"Oh, I was down in the emergency department an hour ago for stomach pain and I overheard some guy on the phone saying he kicked you in the back and your head started bleeding. Did you get in a fight? Why would he do that?" She asked.

"As far as your woman; who cares?" I leaned on the wall looking at her bend down to try and kiss him. He squeezed her cheeks so tight her lips were like a fish.

"I told you my girl was here and you're still being disrespectful. I don't play that shit and you know it. I suggest you get you get the fuck out." He let her face go and she wiped the tears. I guess he squeezed her face really hard. I went to sit with him on the bed and her eyes got wide when she noticed the ring on my finger.

"Well I guess my child will have a fat, ugly stepmother." She slammed some paper on the bed and stormed out. I picked it up and I'll be damned if she wasn't pregnant. Three months to be exact and that came from looking at the ultrasound. We weren't together when he slept with her but I'm not dealing with another baby mother.

"Isa." I stood up.

"Leave me alone Birch." I pulled the chair out and extended it to a bed. I put the sheet and blanket on it the nurse gave me and went to lie down.

"Isa, take the bed. I'll lay there."

"It's fine Birch."

"Take the damn bed Isa. Shit. I know you're mad but you're pregnant." He moved over to the chair thing and I got in the bed. I handed him the remote, the nurses button and anything else I thought he needed. I could see he was in pain and left the room to ask the nurse to bring him something. Hopefully, it will put him to sleep so he doesn't talk to me. The nurse came in, took his vitals and gave him medication.

"Isa."

"I don't want to talk about it Brayden. Please just let me go to sleep."

"How are you going to sleep if you're over there crying?"

"I'll be fine." I grabbed some tissues and wiped my face.

50

"FUCKKKKK!" I heard him shout. I didn't turn around or ask if he was ok. He's lucky I stayed after she dropped that bomb.

****

Over the next few days I stayed at the hospital with him and his mom brought the kids up. I still had no words for him and everyone could tell something was going on but no one asked. It was his business to tell so when he was ready; he could. The doctor came in and said all his test were good and he could go home tomorrow. At least I had more space to be away from him there.

Birch

I don't know how shit keeps going from bad to worse. Abel's punk ass snuck me from behind and I ended up in the hospital for a week. Lira came on some bullshit about being pregnant and I'm not sure if it's true. Well it's definitely true according to the discharge papers. I only slept with her unprotected once and it was really to make up for the night I fucked her when I was mad at Isa and she bled. I went to her house a few days after it happened and we both were drinking, one thing led to another and we had sex on the couch and I regretted it the next day when I realized we didn't use one. I asked her to get the pill and she promised she would but here I am sitting in my home office with the pregnancy results and an ultrasound she couldn't wait to show Isa.

I give it to my girl though. She stayed with me the entire week after Lira dropped the papers off. She may not have said two words to me but her presence was enough. Now, I've been home for a week and she still has yet to speak to me. She did start working at the office where we had the condominiums built and went to work faithfully. Once she came home dinner was made, she spent time with the kids, got them ready for bed and slept in the guest room where I wouldn't see her until the next morning. I'm sure she's hurting; hell I'm hurting for her because me being childish, I have three kids on the way and I only want the one Isa is carrying. It may sound harsh but it's reality. I will love all my kids but damn. I may not have been with Isa at the time the kids were conceived with Lira and Lique but I knew better.

"Brayden wants to talk to you on the phone. He said he's been calling but you haven't answered." Isa said peeking in my office.

"Isa." I called out to her, as she was about to close the door.

"Call your son. I'm dropping the kids off at daycare. Have a good day."

"Got dammit Isa, talk to me. What the fuck?" I shouted running after her.

"I don't have anything to say Brayden. We weren't together when you had sex with those women. I have nothing to do with what you have going on." I ran my hand down my face.

"You're right but say something to me. Tell me how upset you are or if you're going to leave me. What's going on in your head? You think this is only affecting you but it's not. I'm a man who's going to

52

take care of my responsibilities but you need to let me know if this is what you want?" I pointed back and forth.

"Or are you going to bounce." She grabbed her purse and keys.

"You want me to speak to you, huh? For what Birch? You need to hear that I accepted a proposal from a man who knew it was a possibility another woman could be bearing his child and never told me. Or do you want to hear how both of your baby mothers are going to cause a lot of drama and I'm not sure I can handle it? Wait, maybe you want to hear me cry at night because I just can't seem to get a man to love me and only me."

"Isa you-" She put her hand up.

"You wanted me to talk to you right?" I nodded my head.

"I go to work everyday with intentions of talking to you when I get home but then I see your face and the mistakes you made, are all I see. I hate for us not to talk and lay up like we used to but I can't right now. Lique is your sons' mother so I can see you sleeping with her unprotected but Lira. You didn't even know her but then again our first time was the same."

"It wasn't like that."

"It doesn't matter. I had to go down to the clinic to get checked and make sure you didn't bring me back anything. DO YOU KNOW HOW FUCKING EMBARRASSING THAT IS? DO YOU?" She was breaking down in front of me and my heart was doing the same.

"I'm sorry Isa." She laughed and wiped her face.

"You always are. Have a good day." She slammed the door behind her and left me standing there.

I sat on the couch and laid my head back. I felt small hands on my face and looked up to see Katarina smiling and asking what time they were going to daycare. Isa was so upset she forgot them. I asked if she wanted to stay home with me but she said no; today was a kid's birthday and she wanted to bring the present her mommy let her buy. Abel could care less if he went but I dropped him off too.

I went over to Lique's place to see my son whom I hadn't since the hospital. My mom brought him over here because Lique claimed to have missed him. *Yea ok.*

"What's up man? Why didn't you go to school today?" I asked when he opened the door. I knew he was home because he text me. I had my phone off until Isa mentioned it. Lira was already driving me crazy and Isa was right because one of my baby mama's is

53

definitely causing drama already.

"Mommy said I had to stay home and take care of her. She isn't feeling well. Dad I don't want to be here with her."

"Where is she?"

"In her room."

"Go get your stuff." He ran off and I made my way to her room. She was in the new condo's we had built. It was decorated nice but then again Lique didn't do cheap. I opened the door and she was coming out the shower with a towel wrapped around her.

"Why is my son at home taking care of you?" She jumped and the towel came unraveled but didn't fall.

"I wanted him to be around me Birch, damn. Can't a mother want to be around her kid?"

"Yea, but not you." I looked around her room and saw a pair of men shoes and clothes.

"Who in the bathroom Lique?" Her eyes got real big.

"Birch our son is here. Don't do this."

"Who is it Lique?" She started crying like a big ass baby.

"You had my son here while another nigga is occupying your time. If you weren't pregnant, I'd beat the shit out of you." I tried to get in the bathroom but she kept blocking me. I turned around and told my son to get in the car. She came down the steps yelling.

"You laid up with that fat bitch and you're questioning me." I yoked her up by the neck.

"That's my fucking fiancé; not some random bitch. She loves Brayden like he's her own son and treats him ten times better than you. The woman you keep treating like shit is the same one telling your son to spend more time with you and even told him to invite your petty ass over, since we'll be a blended family. You can't seem to get passed her looks when in actuality she will always be a beautiful woman in my eyes, inside and out." I saw tears rolling down her face.

"A bad bitch doesn't make a good woman. Once all the makeup and tight clothes come off, that same insecure and low self esteem woman is still there; remember that." I let her neck go and walked to the door. She was crying her eyes out. I guess a nigga hit home with my words but she needed to hear it.

"Dad, can I live with you permanently?" My son asked when we pulled off.

"You already know." We gave each other a pound. I took him to school and went to pick something up to take Isa for lunch. I hate

that we're on bad terms but she's still my fiancé and pregnant.
****

"Why won't you answer when I call?" I turned around to see Lira standing there smirking. This bitch had on some tight jeans and a fitted shirt.

"I didn't know pregnant people wore tight clothes. And until we know for sure that's my kid, there's no need for you to call me non stop the way you have." Her smirk turned to a frown real quick.

"Oh, I guess the ugly stepmom is having a problem." I chuckled and ordered my food. Lira was about to have me choke the shit out of her. She as well as everyone else knows I don't play when it comes to Isa but they stayed testing me. I ignored her and waited for my food.

"Sir you didn't pay." The cashier said as I tried to pick my bag up.

"I paid the lady right there." I pointed and the lady confirmed it.

"Oh, but the lady you were speaking with said you were paying for hers." The woman spoke with and attitude and folded her arms. When the hell did Lira tell her that and how long was she really here?

"First of all… don't give me no fucking attitude over the dumb shit you did." Her mouth dropped open.

"Second… you should've checked with me first, before assuming what she said was true. I'm sure people come here and speak to others all the time but it doesn't make it their responsibility to pay for them. And third… you must be outta your fucking mind if you think I'm paying for some random chicks food."

I snatched my bag and the manager came walking out asking what the problem was. When I told him what she did, he apologized and gave me one of those cards where if you buy a certain amount of food, the next one is free. I will use it but not when she's working. Isa and Maylan showed me what angry people do to food, so I'm good. I sent Lira a text cursing her the hell out and blocked her. I didn't have time for the games she playing when I got my own shit going on.

I parked in front of Isa's job and grabbed the food. As I stepped in, I heard some giggling and saw a nigga standing in front of her desk. It was some dude who looked like he was flirting with her and she got a kick out of it.

"Aye. She has a man bro." I lifted her hand up and showed off her ring.

"Ugh so do I. She isn't my type. I apologize for putting a smile on her face. Damn girl this man is fine." He said and I almost knocked him the hell out. He ran out the office fast as hell.

"What do you want Birch?" She sat in her chair.

"I brought my fiancé lunch." She rolled her eyes but took the bag out my hand and smiled when she looked inside. I brought her favorite cheesesteak with fries.

"Thank you." She put a fry in her mouth as she stood and placed a kiss on my lips. I was happy she did that being we haven't spoken to one another in days. I grabbed her quick and wrapped my arms around her waist.

"Stop Birch. I'm hungry." She whined reaching for another fry.

"I'm hungry too." I placed kisses on her neck and let my hands unbutton her pants. My fingers circled her clit and she let a moan slip out.

"I miss you Isa."

"Ssssss Brayden." I felt her knees giving out. Her head was on my shoulder with her hand around my neck.

"Give me a kiss Isa." She let her tongue go in my mouth but I wanted more. I went to the door and locked it.

"Get on the desk and open up."

"No Birch. I-" I walked over, removed all her clothes and made her sit on the desk. I separated her legs and dove right in.

"Damn, I missed eating this good ass pussy. Mmmmm, keep cumming for me Isa." She came so much we were going to need a lot of paper towels to clean up. It took me all of five seconds to undo my jeans and slide in. Her hands were under my shirt digging in my back.

"You know there's no out with me right?" I stared in her eyes waiting for an answer.

"Brayden, I'm not leaving you. I need space to process all of it, that's all. Shittttt baby." Her nectar was covering my dick.

"Good." I pulled out and jerked myself off until I came in my hand.

"What the hell?" She sat up mad.

"When you start speaking to me, I'll let you finish." She pushed me in the chest and I helped her off the desk laughing. After we cleaned her and the office up, I sat there watching television. My mom had a thirty-two inch on the wall from when she worked here. I listened to Isa on the phone and interact with the people who came in. She was a natural and the people loved her.

"What are you doing?" I asked after the last person left. It was almost time to pick the kids up and she locked the door, walking over to me licking her lips.

"About to please my fiancé." She dropped to her knees and topped me off.

"Yo Isa, don't play." She stood up and started getting her things together; leaving me with blue balls.

"Oh, I'm not playing. You want to get that nut, I suggest you handle that before we leave." She smirked and stood there.

"Isa give me a hand job or something." Her hand jobs are just as good as her mouth. My woman is definitely a beast in the bedroom.

"Not at all. Do you need a visual to finish?" She unbuttoned her blouse and began rubbing her breast and licking on them. Fuck it; if this is how I'm going to do it, I may as well enjoy it.

"Brayden, I love the way you suck on my pussy. The way you make me cum over and over. Mmmmm, I can feel you sliding your fingers in and out." She started talking that freaky shit and I lost control.

"Fuck Isaaaaa." She made it to my dick just in time and sucked me off until I had nothing left.

"The things I do for you." She went in the bathroom and I heard her gargling with mouthwash. She always kept a small travel size bottle in her purse, just in case. Yea, we were freaks and wasn't ashamed of it. I walked in behind her and stared in the mirror.

"And I love you even more for it."

"Do you Brayden? I need to know that these kids' parents aren't going to destroy what we have. I'm trying to understand baby, I really am but I'm scared. I can't take another heartbreak."

"I'm not going to hurt you Isa. I messed up and I don't want to lose you. I swear no one is going to come between us and I damn sure ain't having anymore kids unless they're with you." I lifted her chin.

"Do you trust me Isa?" She nodded her head yes.

"Then know, I will never intentionally cause you pain and I'm going to make sure no bullshit comes your way."

"But you'll have to spend time with the babies at their house and I don't want you to get tempted and-"

"I don't need to see my kids there. I will bring them to our house and dare Lira or Lique to try and stop me. I love you Isa. You can't take another heartbreak and I refuse to be the one who gives it to you." We stood there kissing when someone knocked on the door.

"Hey is Isa here?" Maylan asked and kept looking behind her.

"Yea, what's wrong and why do you keep checking behind you?"

"No reason. Can I come in?" I stepped aside and told Isa she was here. At first she wasn't happy but I told her something is wrong with Maylan and if anything happened to her she would regret not speaking to her. I didn't want to leave with Maylan acting scary the way she was but they needed to talk and the kids had to be picked up. I told Maylan to follow Isa home instead. I followed them too; to make sure no one followed her and then went to get the kids. I had to call Vernon because this shit with his baby mama is crazy.

Maylan

I followed Isa home and noticed Birch did the same. I guess me being paranoid and shit, had him nervous. I parked behind her and watched her grab the stuff from the car and head inside. She left the door open and just as I was getting out, my phone rang. It was Jared asking where I was and what time did I plan on returning home. I started my car up and went to his house, which is where I had been staying, unless I had my son with me. I was still staying at my parents' house and refused to go back to the place Vernon brought me. The reason was no longer because I was mad at him but more so, I didn't want Jared to know about it. I wanted to go there to get away but running from my problems wasn't going to do anything for me.

"Where you been?" Jared questioned me when I walked in his house. He had a toothpick hanging out his mouth and a towel wrapped around his waist with water dripping. He was definitely a sexy man but he had a dark side like most niggas and I couldn't get away from him.

"Oh hey." Celeste came from out the bathroom fixing her clothes. My eyes got big as hell. I didn't even know they were associated with each other and when did she start speaking to me.

"What's going on Jared?" He moved in closer to me.

"You don't get to ask me shit. Now answer the fucking question. Where the fuck were you?"

"I went to see Isa but-"

"Didn't I tell you to stay away from that bitch and anyone associated with her?" His fist caught my mouth and I swear a tooth came out as blood spilled from it. Another one caught the side of my face and now he had me by the neck squeezing the life out of me. I saw a smirk on Celeste face. I know she's getting a kick out of it because she'd have Vernon if I were dead. I clawed at him over and over but he wouldn't let go. It didn't faze him being two of my fingers were already broken and my neck was still sore from the last time. I really didn't have the strength to fight back and he knew it. The black eye had just healed and I'm probably going to have another one.

"Yo, motherfucker what you doing?" Some guy came from upstairs. He had a blunt in his mouth and his shirt was off. Some chick came behind him and had her mouth covered.

"This doesn't concern you." Jared told him staring in my eyes. Its like he wanted to see my soul leave my body.

"The hell if it don't. Nigga let her the fuck go. You aren't about to take her life while I'm here. " I felt Jared's releasing my neck and my body hit the floor. I heard the two of them arguing.

"Why didn't you let him kill her?" I heard Celeste ask as I gasped for air. The chick that came out with the guy came running over to me.

"Are you ok?" I told her yes, once I was able to speak.

"What the hell is wrong with you and are you trying to kill her?" She asked Jared who was staring at me like I'm the one in the wrong.

"And so what if he were." Celeste said and folded her arms.

"Bitch, who asked you." The unknown guy snapped.

"Bitch." She asked him sarcastically.

"You heard me."

"Baby, let me get this for you." The girl left me sitting there and walked over to Celeste.

"Listen boo. I'm not sure who you are, nor do I care but that man right there." She pointed to the guy, who I have yet to know his name and thank him for saving me.

"I'm his wife and anything you have to say to him, I'm right here. He may not hit a bitch, but I'll knock one the fuck out." She removed her earrings and Celeste looked scared, which is surprising. I don't know what happened after that because Jared picked me up and carried me in the bedroom, slamming the door behind him.

"Go in the bathroom and clean yourself up." He waved me off and I closed the bathroom door and did what he told me. Two of my teeth on the left hand side were gone and my eye was swelling up but not to where it would close. My neck had hella marks on it. I don't know how I got here but one thing I do know for sure is I need to get as far away from him as possible. I stood in the shower reminiscing on how things were perfect in the beginning but the tell tale signs were there and it started the day in the mall when he tried to snatch me up. I should've listened to Dante when he said shit wouldn't turn out right if I messed with this dude and he was using me.

Jared was the perfect gentleman at first besides the issue at the mall. He wined and dined me and swooped me off my feet. He was the perfect distraction from Vernon and I's problems.

60

However, after the first couple of weeks, I noticed his attitude changing whenever I would mention picking my son up or his father dropping him off. He didn't want me anywhere near Vernon and forbid me to contact him. If anything needed to be discussed about my son, I had to go through his mom. He alienated me from Isa, the kids and if it had not been my son was a newborn, he'd probably make me do the same with him. Its only been a few months since we've been together but the pain he had inflicted on me thus far, would make someone believe we've been around one another for years.

In the entire time I was with Vernon, he never even thought about laying hands on me. Yes, we had problems when it came to his ex but he always put me first. If only I'd listened to Dante and acted like a woman and talked to Vernon, I wouldn't be in this situation. I wanted badly to tell Isa what was going on because I knew she'd tell Vernon and he'd save me but she refused to speak with me and I understood. I missed a lot of important moments with her because of my attitude and I haven't seen Dawn's son with Dante because of it as well. The only time Jared gave me space was when I had my son and even then, I think he had someone following me. I was only able to see Isa tonight because I was dropping VJ off to his grandmother but he called and summoned me here, only to see Celeste come out looking guilty. Its like she got a kick out of seeing me hurt and I don't know why?

I stared in the mirror crying as I rinsed my mouth out. It was a lot of blood and it took a while for me to get the bleeding under control. I put two cotton balls in my mouth and turned the shower on. I ended up using the bathroom on myself when he tried to choke me so when I took my clothes off, I tossed them in the trash. I stepped in and my neck began to sting from the open scratches from his nails. I let the water hit my face and it hurt like hell too, I guess the water was harder than I thought.

I heard the bathroom door open as I continued washing up and felt him step in behind me. I let the tears fall as he ran his fingers up and down my bottom half. He placed kisses on my back and all I wanted to do was jump out. I heard him whispering how sorry he was but was he really? Its not like this is the first and I'm sure not the last time he put hands on me. My body was swung around and I prayed to God he didn't notice me crying. His lips touched mine and I hated what was going to happen next.

I felt his tongue sliding across my lips and at the same time he lifted my legs up and thrusted himself inside of me. I kept telling him to stop; we needed a condom but he pretended not to hear me. The last few times we had sex, he refused to use one. After a few minutes of hearing him say how good the pussy is and I better not be with anyone else or he'll kill me; he came inside of me.

He let my feet down and told me to go down on him and yes my first instinct was to bite his dick off but he made it very clear what would happen if I tried anything funny. I felt his hand on my head as I bobbed up and down on him. His dick started to twitch, which let me now he was about to let go. I never swallowed for him but today he held my head there and made me. I vomited all over the shower because it was disgusting. Vernon's sperm had a light salty taste but I loved tasting him, but Jared's was different and I didn't like it. He yanked me up by my hair and ran the tip of his dick across my clit and in no time entered me again. I swear if it weren't for the water from the shower, he'd be having dry sex with me.

"Fuck Maylan, this pussy is so got damn good." I rolled my eyes and waited for him to finish. The shower curtain opened slowly and Celeste stood there recording us having sex.

"What the fuck are you doing?" I asked and tapped Jared.

"Yea baby." I tried to move but he wouldn't let go.

"Jared stop. Why is she recording us?"

"I told her too."

"WHAT?" I yelled out and kept smacking him to stop. He yanked my hair back and made me look at him. He stuck his tongue in my mouth. I pulled back and he wrapped his hands on my throat again. I felt his body shake and he came again, inside me.

"Yea. I just fucked the shit out of Maylan bro. I can see why you won't leave her alone." He smacked me on the ass a few times and looked in the camera.

"Jared are you fucking crazy?" He slapped me so hard I fell against the shower and slid down.

"Make sure you save that so we can send it to him when the time is right." I heard him say as he stepped out.

"I told you I would get Vernon back and this right here is going to do it." Celeste said and walked out the bathroom. I let out a scream and sat there letting the water hit my body. I don't know how long I was there but the chick came in the bathroom and helped me get out.

"Who are you and why are you helping me?" She lifted my chin and smiled.

"Jared is my cousin and I came to visit. My husband and I are looking to move and he said this was a great area. The reason I'm helping you is because he did the same thing to his ex and lets just say she didn't make it out." I covered my mouth.

"Are you saying he killed her?"

"That's exactly what I'm saying. Come on, let's gets you dressed." She gave me a towel and followed me in the room.

"But how is he here?"

"Honey, money makes the world go round. Somehow his lawyer got him off claiming self-defense. He had scratches on him and the judge was related to the lawyer and you know how that goes."

"I may not be smart but I do know they shouldn't have been on the case together."

"Bingo. But like I said money talks, bullshit walks."

"Do you have anyone you can stay with or-" I shook my head no.

"My best friend won't speak to me because when she needed me, I was acting like a brat. My son's father is not going to have anything to do with me once Celeste shows him that video."

"What video?" I gave her a crazy look.

"She came in and taped Jared and I having unwanted sex in the shower and when I asked him about it, he said he told her to do it. After we were done he looked in the camera and taunted him. I asked was he crazy and he backhanded me, which is why you found me the way you did."

"I told my husband we shouldn't have left you alone."

"Huh?"

"After I almost beat the shit out of that chick, Dave took me outside and we ended up going to the store. When we came back no one was here but I heard the shower going."

"Wait, you have a key? How long have you been in town?"

"We got here this morning an my husband is ready to go already. I talked him into staying at a hotel until we got the chance to look around."

"Well, I thank you and your husband for saving me but I'm pretty much stuck here." I followed her in the living room. Her husband was on the phone talking to someone and hung up when he saw us.

"You good." He asked and looked at his wife. I swear Vernon used to look at me the same way. I could see the love they had for each other and wanted the same thing.

"Thank you."

"I'm not going to ask why you're still with this nigga because its evident you're scared but you have to get away from him or I hate to say it, but you will suffer the same fate as the last chick."

"Babe, I just told her the same thing but she has no one."

"What you mean? Everybody has someone, whether it's who she wants to be with or not, we all have somebody."

"I had a support system but my attitude made them stop fucking with me and honestly, I don't want to hear the I told you so's. I'm going to get away from him soon, but right now, I have to figure out what he wants from my sons father?"

"Hold up. I know you're not enduring this pain to get information." Her husband stood up.

"No I'm not. I didn't know he wanted anything to do with my son's father until today. I figured the video is collateral for something and I hope I find out sooner than later."

"That's what gets a woman killed. You're going to stay here a little longer in hopes you can find out some information that your kids' father can probably get. He's probably taunting him to be smart. Its women like you that make people believe a woman who gets beat, deserves the shit."

"Dave." The chick was upset.

"No babe. Here she has a chance right now to bounce since he left and all she's worried about is some information. Your ass is going to be dead fucking with him and I can't say it won't be your fault." He said to his wife and she gave me a sad look.

"Lets go. We saved her once; she has to save herself." And with that he held her hand as they walked out. I heard everything he said, loud and clear but I couldn't let Vernon die either. I pray Jared slips up soon.

Vernon

I've been losing my damn mind ever since I saw the way Maylan looked at the hospital. She won't answer her phone and she somehow seems to drop my son off and pick him up when I'm not there. It's as if she knows I'm going to question her. Birch told me the other day she came looking for Isa at the office and even followed them to the house but when he got back, Isa told him she never came in and left right after he did. I haven't heard from Celeste but I'm sure I will soon, now that I know she gave me the information about Maylan fucking someone else. She probably did it, in hopes I would end up back in bed with her but it won't.

I used to love Celeste but never in a way like Maylan. Don't get me wrong, in the beginning Celeste could have whatever she wanted from me but the constant nagging and accusing me of cheating when at the time I wasn't; became too much. Yea, I cheated a lot but when she asked, I wasn't. No woman ever approached her about our rendezvous but she was insecure as hell and I couldn't take it. I'd break up with her and a few months later we'd get back together but even that got tiring.

That's why when Maylan came around; Celeste hated her for getting me to fall for her even before I got the pussy. There's nothing I wouldn't do for Maylan and she knows it but she told me there were things I needed to deal with first and she was right. The last few times Celeste and I had sex all she spoke about was why I didn't love her the same way. To be honest, to this day, I don't know why I couldn't.

The day Maylan and I spoke in depth at the hospital, I listened to her and could see why she felt the way she did. As much as I hate to say it, Celeste was a fixture in my

life and not for just the sex. She and I had time in and even though she pissed me off, we still had a friendship. I was comfortable talking to her about certain things but when it came to Maylan, it should've been off limits, especially when it came to my son.

I didn't even think when I mentioned the test because it was no secret how I felt about the situation. The crazy part is, when the results came, I refused to open them. Maylan sure as hell didn't have a problem sending me a screen shot of them to me though. I haven't seen Celeste or answered any of her calls since my son was born and it's going to stay that way. Maylan is the only woman I want and when I find her, she'll know.

Today Dante was having a get together at his house because Dawn had the baby and he purchased a house out here to be closer to us. He claimed he didn't trust Abel and felt something was going to happen and he couldn't be here. After the shit with Birch we've been trying to find Abel but his ass went into hiding. It didn't matter because eventually he would show his face. He had a business to run and he would never miss out on money.

We did empty the apartment the girls stayed in and gave the furniture to the good will. Neither Birch nor I brought it but you could tell it was brand new so Abel must've. The apartment was repainted, cleaned up and rented to someone else last week. It was an older couple with two kids who were seven and eight.

"Hey." My mom said when I stopped by to see if Maylan dropped VJ off. I told my mom to tell her I wanted to take him with me.

"Hey. VJ is asleep but let me talk to you for a minute." I followed her in the kitchen and sat down.

"What's up? Is that chicken for Dante's house?" She said yes and popped my hand when I tried to take a piece but I got one anyway. I put some hot sauce on it and grabbed something to drink.

"I think he's beating on her?"

"Who?" She gave me a crazy look.

"Who you talking about? You speak to so many people." I hated when she assumed I could guess who it was. My mom spoke to mad people on a daily basis and expected me to know all of them when she told me their business.

"Maylan." I stopped eating and stared at her.

"I hope you said her name by accident." I licked my fingers, tossed the bone in the trash and washed my hands in the sink. The look on my moms face told me she said the right person.

"What makes you say that?" I dried my hands on the paper towel and opened the water bottle.

"Vernon, she has the signs of a battered woman?"

"Ma, what are the signs?"

"You didn't see her two fingers were broke, or the marks around her neck. I know damn well you saw the black eye."

"I did but it doesn't mean she's being beat on. Ma, you know Maylan has a mouth on her and most likely got in a fight." I didn't want to believe she allowed a man to hit her.

"Vernon, you are my son and I love you but Maylan has become my daughter; regardless if the two of you are together or not. I'm telling you he's hitting her and I'm scared he's going to hurt her real bad; maybe kill her."

"Did you ask her?"

"She denied it and started crying. I asked her if he wasn't, why was she crying and she told me I wouldn't understand. Son, I went to give VJ a kiss and she flinched. I'm telling you something ain't right with her." As she said that my phone vibrated and it was Maylan asking me to meet her somewhere.

I told my mom I would be back to get the food and VJ in an hour. The get together didn't start for a couple of hours anyway. I got out at the restaurant and went inside. Maylan was sitting at a table staring out the window and didn't acknowledge my presence. I sat there staring at her as she wiped the few tears that fell.

"Remember when we used to come here and molest each other under the table?" I laughed at the memory. She and I would have sex anywhere and do things like that whenever we went out.

"Yea we did a lot of nasty things to each other." She chuckled and turned to look at me and I almost lost my fucking mind. She had another black eye, fresh marks on her neck and when she gave me that fake smile, I could see teeth missing.

"What happened to you?" I asked as calm as I could.

"I'm ok Vernon. I asked you here because I need you to keep VJ for a while."

"WHAT?"

"I have some things going on and."

"Is he putting his hands on you May?" She was about to answer.

"Hey baby. I've been looking for you." The dude Jared said to her. I remembered him from the night in the club.

"I needed to speak to Vernon. I didn't hear my phone." He reached his hand out for her and she looked petrified.

"Maylan, tell me right now if he did this to you. I swear to God, I'll kill his ass." Her lip started trembling and it took her a minute to answer but she told me no.

"Man, I don't put my hands on women. Two chicks at the mall jumped Maylan. Right babe?"

"Thanks for meeting me Vernon." I stood up when she did.

"Maylan, you don't have to go with him."

"Vernon he didn't do it. I'm going with him because I don't want you two arguing or fighting over something that isn't true."

"You heard her man."

"Bye Vernon." For some reason it felt like the way she said it, meant forever.

"Don't worry about her Vernon. Daddy is taking very good care of her." He squeezed her ass while they walked out.

"Yo my man let me give her a hug first." He turned around and I saw his face turn up. He nodded at Maylan and she came over to me and wrapped her arms around me tight. Her entire body was trembling and she kissed my cheek.

"Tell Isa, I'm sorry for missing out on her big moments and I'm so happy for her. Vernon, tell VJ I love him and I never meant to leave him. Take care of him and raise him right." She patted me on the chest.

"Maylan what the fuck?"

"Bye Vernon and please don't make things worse than they are. VJ needs you and I can't go on knowing something happened to you too. I made my bed and now I have to lie in it. I love you." She let my hand go and walked away.

"MAYLAN!" I shouted and she never turned around. I ran out behind her and dude had his gun to my face.

"Vernon please just go." I was pissed my gun was in the car.

"Yea Vernon go." He said mocking her.

"Maylan you know this shit don't scare me. Come with me and I swear he won't bother you." I saw her look at him and then take a small step to me but he pulled her back.

"Listen here partner. Maylan belongs to me now. You had your chance with her and fucked up. She doesn't want you and to show you, I had your ex Celeste send something to your phone."

"Celeste."

"Oh yea, that's the bitch you allowed to interfere in your relationship, which is how I got to her but never fear. Jared is going to take real good care of Maylan; especially now that I purposely got her pregnant." Maylan's swung her head around as if what he said was a surprise to her. He walked backwards to his car and I stared down at my phone looking at the video of him fucking her with no condom. I could tell she was upset over the video but the sound was removed. I cut it off and walked up to the car they were getting in.

"Maylan you let him fuck you raw?" Now I was pissed.

"Vernon it wasn't like that. Please just go. You're making it worse antagonizing him."

"I'm antagonizing him now because I was trying to save your life. You know what? Let that nigga whoop your ass, I don't give a fuck."

"Vernon please." She was crying hard and I didn't give a fuck anymore.

"Fuck you Maylan. You want to be with that nigga, then go ahead. Don't call about my son either. I see you making a new life with him so stay the fuck away from me."

"Vernon." I didn't turn around and kept walking to my car. I sat there pissed off when I heard a woman scream. I turned around and she had her mouth covered. I got out to hear what she was talking about since she drew a crowd. I overheard her say, the man who left with the woman in his car punched her so hard, he knocked her out. She saw her in the front seat with her nose bleeding and it looked broke. Someone asked if she was sure and she said yes because her car was next to his and as she got out to go in, he did it. *Damn! What did I do?*

****

"It's about time you got here." Dante said when I walked in with my son and mom. I took the tray in the kitchen and opened the door to the back to get my mind right. The shit the woman said didn't sit right with me and I had to figure out a way to find Maylan.

"Vernon have you seen Maylan? I know I've been a bitch to her but I miss her." Isa said stepping out on the porch with me. I turned around and smiled. I was mean as hell to this woman and she still forgave me. I didn't know how I was going to break the news to her.

"Isa, umm."

"What's up y'all?" Birch came out with Dave, who is Dante's cousin. He lived in Virginia with his wife but came out here to purchase a house. We didn't know him like that but the few times he's been here we chilled with him. He was a businessman himself and his wife was a teacher.

69

"Nothing. What's up Dave?" I slapped hands with him and noticed Isa walking away. At this moment I was happy she did because I had no idea how I would explain what's going on with Maylan to her. Birch gave me a look and I told him we would discuss it later.

Dawn brought the baby out and all the women cooed over him and the other kids were running through the house. Her parents were there and we assumed they would be racists or stuck up but they were down to earth and her mom held VJ the entire time and kept saying how chunky he was. My mom asked me if I heard from Maylan and I told her no but that I did see her. I also told my mom if she wanted help she had to reach out. No one could make her do what she didn't want to.

Dante

"Hey baby. You good." I asked Dawn who sat at the table looking stressed out.

"Dante, today is not the time for the bullshit and how in the hell did she know where we lived?" She stood up to walk away but I grabbed her hand.

"Who?" She showed me her phone and it was a message from someone telling her to come outside so they could fight her.

"Who is this?"

"I'm assuming its Kacey." She went to the door and sure enough the bitch was standing on my front lawn.

"Dante let that bitch out."

"Bitch. Who the fuck you talking to?" I moved towards her and I felt someone pull me back.

"What do you want Kacey?" Dawn asked and stood on the front porch.

"I want you. You thought I forgot about the smack and how you maced me in the mall parking lot. Nah bitch. Now that you had the baby, its time to pay up."

"How did she know I had the baby?" Kacey started laughing.

"Oh your man told me when we were together the other night." Dawn's head swung around so fast, I thought it would snap. By now people were coming out the door to find out what was going on.

"Bitch, stop making it seem like we were alone. Dawn, I saw her at the bar when me and Vernon went out for drinks. She overheard me and him talking about today. I don't know how she found out where we lived."

"Don't lie Dante. You know I had your dick in my mouth in the bathroom." I saw Dawn's face turn up and something triggered inside me. I took off running to Kacey and tried to kill that bitch. Not only was she lying but she had my girl crying and embarrassed the hell out of her. I kicked Kacey in her stomach and hoped she lost the baby that she claimed to be pregnant with. The guys pulled me off her. I walked to the door and my girl had a disgusted look on her face.

"I'm done Dante. I can't do this anymore." She said and made her way in the house and ran up the stairs.

"Dawn, I swear she's lying."

"I don't even care anymore Dante. I'm tired of the bullshit with her and if this is how we're going to live the rest of our life, I don't want it. The kids were out there, heard her call me names and say their dad allowed another woman to touch him. Kristopher and Asha are old enough to know exactly what she means."

"Dawn, listen to me." I snatched the clothes out her hand she was trying to throw in a suitcase.

"She followed me in the bathroom and tried, I'm not going to lie but she didn't get my clothes down. I pushed her against the wall and choked the shit out of her. I would've killed her, had Vernon not come in. He saw her follow me and came to make sure I was good."

"Vernon is your best friend; do you really think I would believe him?"

"Dawn, you're not leaving me." I tossed the suitcase on the other side of the room and threw her against the door but not hard.

"I swear on my newborn son, I didn't allow her to touch me. You're going to believe what you want and that's fine but the only way you're leaving me, is if you're dead."

"Dante." I could see how scared she was.

"I'm tired of this shit with Kacey and I'm going to handle it."

"You can't make me stay here."

"You heard what the fuck I said Dawn. If you even think about trying to leave me, I will find you." I opened the door and left her standing there crying.

I grabbed my keys and heard Vernon tell his mom he'd be back and to stay there. It didn't take long for Birch to jump in the car. He was on the phone with Smitty telling him we'd be back and to make sure Isa and the kids stayed there. My phone rang from Dawn over and over but I refused to answer it. I meant what I said about her not leaving me. If I had to find Kacey, kill her and show Dawn the body, I would. Fortunately, for Kacey, I couldn't find her and I checked everywhere for over two hours. I stopped at the bar because I needed a damn drink.

"What the fuck is going on? It seems like every bit of drama in our life is linked back to Abel or his crew." Birch said and tossed back a drink.

"Maylan is getting her ass beat by dude and today Celeste sent me a video of him fucking her raw in the shower. I couldn't take it and blacked out on her in front of him. Never mind the fact he claimed to have gotten her pregnant on purpose." Vernon said tossing back the three shots he ordered.

Birch and I both sat there not saying a word. He then told us how she asked him to keep the baby and made sure he grew up right. The kicker was him mentioning some lady saying the man in the car knocked her out. I could see the stress all over his face but I agree with him when he said, *"If she wanted the help she had to ask."* Vernon would have never allowed her to leave with him if she just said the word.

"What the fuck you want?" I heard Vernon say when he saw Celeste come take a seat next to him.

"I just wanted to check on you."

"How did you know I was here and why did you send me that video?" We waited for her to answer.

"He made me. He said if I didn't, he would kill you and regardless of you not wanting me, I don't want anything to happen to you." She ran her hand down his face and he moved away.

"Where is he Celeste?"

"I don't know." She ordered a drink and got comfortable. Vernon snatched her off the seat and they went to the back. I can guess what he's about to do. Birch and I sat there talking about getting Abel. He had a lot of shit going and needed to be dealt with. Vernon came out ten minutes later with a grin on his face.

"Damn, that was quick." I looked for Celeste and didn't see her.

"Lets go." Birch paid the tab and we left.

"What happened in the bathroom? Please don't tell me you fucked her." I said glancing in my rearview at him in the backseat.

"Nah, but I let her suck my dick."

"Mannnnn, you have got to leave her alone."

"Oh she gave me dude's address to where he has Maylan."

"Why did she do that?"

"I told her we could work on us but that's never happening." He gave me the address and sat quiet the entire ride. We parked and knocked on the door but no one answered. Birch asked if he saw her car but it wasn't there. Vernon kicked it open and we all searched the house. Maylan was nowhere in sight.

I called out for him so we could bounce before dude came home but he didn't answer. Birch and I looked at each other and ran up the steps. He was on the floor holding Maylan's lifeless body in his arms; crying.

"Yo, call an ambulance." I picked the phone up and dialed 911. Birch found a sheet to throw over her because she was naked with blood all over her.

"Maylan baby, please wake up. Fuckkk, why didn't I just make you leave with me? Come on Maylan, get up. VJ needs you to make it and so do I." This nigga had me and Birch shedding a few tears seeing him broken like this. The EMT's got there fast as hell.

"Sir you have to let her go so we can get her to the hospital." He kissed her lips and let go.

"Oh my God, what happened to her?" We all ran downstairs to see who the woman was yelling. It was Dante's cousin and his wife.

"Yo, what are y'all doing here?" Dave asked. Vernon told the EMT's he was riding with them and dared them to say no.

"We came to check on her." Dave started telling us what he saw Jared do to her and told Maylan she needed to leave but she refused because she wanted to know why he wanted Vernon. I know he was going to be mad once he found out she stayed for him. His wife felt like something was wrong and that's why they came here. She was hysterical crying and asked Dave to take her to the hospital.

Birch and I stayed behind to search his house. We came up with nothing but Maylan's phone and a manila envelope. Inside the envelope was papers about him being arrested and beating a murder charge against his previous girlfriend. The photos of her body were similar to the ones Maylan had. She had stab wounds on her chest, her eyes were swollen shut, her arm was dislocated and he even cut all her hair off. He didn't cut Maylan's but there was a pair of scissors on the dresser, which made us think he was about to but knew we were there and had most likely just left.

We grabbed the folder and left the house. We both said we weren't going to tell Dawn or Isa until we heard from Vernon because they would have a fit. Isa is due in 5 weeks and Dawn just had my son a month ago.

"Yo, what they saying?" I asked when we got to the hospital. Birch and I both told our women we were still at the bar drinking. Isa told him to hurry up because she was ready to go home and Dawn told me to fuck off. Little did she know I was fucking her off, when I got home.

"I don't know yet. Man, I don't think she's going to make it. There was so much blood and she kept flat lining on the way."

"Damn. Maybe we should call her-"

"HELL FUCKING NO! The last time something happened to her, her mom wouldn't tell me shit. I told them she's my wife and I'm her only family member and it's staying that way."

"Alright man." I sat down next to him and Birch did the same. After two hours Vernon asked us to leave and he would contact us when he heard something. At first we wouldn't but he said he needed to be alone. We got to the house and everyone was gone except Isa and the kids. They were asleep upstairs so I told them to let the kids stay.

"Come here Dawn." I yelled out while I was in the shower.

"What?" She leaned on the door with an attitude.

"Get your ass over here."

"No Dante. I'm over this nonsense and." I jumped out the shower and pushed her against the wall. Both of my arms were placed on the side of her head on the wall.

"Move." I stared at her and placed my mouth or hers, removed her shorts and plunged inside her forcefully. We weren't supposed to have sex for another two weeks but she had to be taught a lesson and I'm just the man to teach her. I lifted her legs and wrapped them around my waist as I dug deeper. Her nails dug in my back and her teeth were in my shoulder.

"Talk that shit about leaving me now Dawn." She squeezed me tighter as she released. I walked in the bedroom still inside her, laid her on the bed, placed her legs on my shoulder and had her begging me to stop.

"Nah, you want to leave me right."

"Dante, oh my God baby. I'm not leaving." I flipped her over on all fours and did circles in her pussy like I was stirring food. She was extremely wet and the sound had me gone.

"Dante baby. Shittttt." She had her back arched gripping the sheets with one hand and digging her nails in my thigh with the other one.

"You leaving me Dawn."

"No baby, no. Here I cummmmmm." She screamed out so loud, I had to cover her mouth. I leaned down on her back and bit gently on her earlobe.

"I'm about to nut all up in this pussy. Fuck baby, you feel so good. Stop trying to take it away. Ahhh damn." I squirted all I had in her and fell on the side of the bed. I pulled her on top of me and made her look at me.

"Baby, I would never cheat on you again and I mean that shit. Stop letting what she says get to you. She wants what you have and every time you get upset she thinks it will make you leave me and I'll go back to her."

"But-"

"But nothing Dawn. You're giving her too much power over our relationship. As far as her knowing where we live, I have no idea but I'm going to find out." She nodded her head. I tried to get some more pussy but she said I fucked her too rough and she was sore.

"I have to tell you something." I told her after we got out the shower and in the bed. I had my hand behind my head as she laid on my chest.

"What's wrong?" I ran my hand down my face. Vernon sent me a text and told me to tell her. When I told her she wanted to go up to the hospital but we didn't have anyone to watch the kids and she damn sure wasn't leaving the house alone this late at night. I told her to call her mom in the morning and see if she could watch the kids. Birch already sent me a message that his mom would pick their kids up early in the morning. He hadn't told Isa yet because he felt she would stress herself out. At least if she were in the hospital, that would be the best place for her.

"How is Vernon?" Dawn asked wiping her eyes.

"He's not doing good but Barry, Smitty and Maria are up there with him now. Tomorrow they'll go home when we get there."

"You guys are taking shifts?"

"Yes. You ok with that?"

"I may not stay up there but I'll be there."

"He knows you just had a baby. Sometimes your presence is enough for someone." I kissed her forehead and had a hard time falling asleep. Believe it or not Maylan's lifeless body made me think about what if it was Dawn? I can't imagine what he's going through and honestly, I don't want to.

Vernon

"Are you the husband of Mrs. Moore?" I told him yes and he brought me in the room. I had everyone come in with me for support. It was seven in the morning by the time the doctor came out to speak. My mom came to the hospital and left VJ at the house with my stepfather. I call him that since he's been around forever and he loved my son. Even though they went married he still called her his wife.

"Mrs. Moore suffered five stab wounds in her chest area, one just missing her heart." My mom covered her mouth. I told her Maylan got hurt but never to what extent.

"Her elbow was dislocated, she had a few cracked ribs and her eyes are completely shut. She is missing seven of her top teeth and a few on the bottom. She will need a dentist to remove some of the others that are either cracked or loose." I put my head down and listened to him finish talking.

"Her blood work came back and she has gonorrhea and chlamydia." I popped my head up. It only confirmed he had sex with her unprotected and gave her diseases. The other STD test came back negative but the HIV test takes a few days.

"Why was there and HIV test taken?" I asked.

"Sir, when a woman comes in brutally attacked the way she did and has an STD, we have to run all tests on her. Its for her safety as well as the staff working with her."

"Was she raped?" I hated to hear the answer but I needed to know.

"No it doesn't appear that she was but she did miscarry."

"How far was she?" I asked with my hands in front of my mouth as my elbows rested on my knees.

"Maybe a couple of weeks." I felt bad she miscarried but she didn't need a baby by him anyway. They didn't give her a DNC as he says because the pregnancy was early and would run its course. It won't prevent her from having kids in the future, either.

"Mrs. Moore is in recovery but will be transported to ICU. She is in a medically induced coma. She had a lot of blood loss and had she not gotten here when she did, she wouldn't be here." My mom patted me on the shoulder.

"Here is the number to the detective who didn't want to bother you. He thinks the person who did this to your wife is wanted elsewhere and he believes, it may be the guy they've been looking for." I took the card, shook his hand and asked if we could see Maylan. He told us to wait until she was brought in the room.

After another hour passed he came back and allowed all of us to go in her room. He let us know that only two people were allowed in the room but he would give us a few minutes to be alone with her, as a family. I felt my knees get weak when I saw all the bandages and machines on her.

"Jesus." I heard my mom say and her and Maria started crying.

"Can y'all give me a minute?" I stood there with my hands in my pockets staring at the woman I planned on spending the rest of my life with, fighting for her life. I pulled the chair up next to her and sat there with her hand in mine. All I wanted to do was marry her, have more kids and live the good life with her by my side and it's been nothing but bullshit the entire time from my ex. I don't care what Celeste says, she knows what happened and I'm going to make her ass pay.

"Maylan, I don't know if you can hear me but baby I'm sorry for everything. I'm sorry for disrespecting our relationship, I'm sorry for getting angry when I saw the video and most of all, I'm sorry for not saving you. I should've seen the signs but you stayed away from me. I don't blame you because I hurt you but you could've come to me and I would've made sure he never touched you." I wiped my nose that was running as I cried talking to her.

"Dammit Maylan, you are so stubborn and I know its why you didn't ask anyone for help. I need you to wake up and tell me you'll be my wife. I promise to never break your heart again or allow anyone to come in between us. I want you to have more of my babies. I need you to wake up baby, please." I felt someone rubbing my back and it was my mom and Birch's mom. One of them handed me tissues to wipe my face.

"She's going to make it Vernon and just know she heard you." Maria said. I guess they all walked in when I was talking, after I told them to stay outside. They don't listen well.

"I don't know ma. Look at her and-" She hugged me and I found myself crying more. How could I not protect her? We all stayed in the room but no one said a word. It was like everyone was in their own thoughts.

"OH MY GOD! WHAT HAPPENED TO HER?" Isa screamed out when she came in and ran over to the bed. Everyone looked at her crying and asking God why did he let someone do that to her. I could see Birch getting upset because she was.

"Pass me that chair for her." Birch yelled out to Smitty. He had Isa sit down and asked the nurse to come check on her. Isa was shaking and shit. I know how bad it was hurting me to see Maylan this way so I can only imagine what its like for her. This is her sister, her best friend, and her kids' godmother. My mom passed her some water and made her drink it. The nurse came in, took her vitals and said her pressure was very high and if seeing her friend this way is too much, its best for her to leave. Isa told the nurse she was fine and refused to move. I looked up and couldn't believe my eyes, but then again, this is what she does.

"Is this bitch fucking crazy?" I said and everyone looked in the direction I was. Celeste stood there trying to look in the room. Smitty shut the blinds they had on the window to watch Maylan and I went out there.

"What the fuck are you doing here and how did you know she was here?" I had a death grip on her arm.

"Jared said he thought someone broke in his house. He saw a lot of blood and Maylan was gone." I stood there staring at her and she was lying. I took her in the hallway and Dante followed me.

"You must think I'm stupid Celeste."

"Vernon I'm not lying. I came up here to support you."

"Get the fuck out of here and if I find out you had anything to do with this, its lights out for you."

"Vernon, is that how you treat the mother of your would be kid?" I chuckled at her. Birch told me about the paper she dropped off confirming her pregnancy I yoked her up and pushed her in the bathroom.

"Celeste, I knew all about you being pregnant because your pussy felt different and after being in Maylan's and she was pregnant, I noticed the difference. That beat down I gave you was on purpose." She covered her mouth.

"I wasn't sure if it was my kid or not. I know for a fact I've never run up in you raw but if you were pregnant, it meant you did something to the condoms. I wasn't about to let you hurt Maylan anymore than you already had, by having a kid by me. You caused enough problems and that would've added to it. Plus, you hate kids and I couldn't take the chance of you harming my kid the way you did Isa's."

79

"Vernon it was a baby."

"And Isa's daughter was four when you did that to her."

"But it was still a baby you beat out of me."

"Yup and now its not. The only baby I have, is my son and when she gets better I'm putting another one in her." I was careful to not tell her too much.

"She's probably already pregnant." She laughed. I guess trying to hurt me.

"She is and I'm going to make sure the kid has my last name and I'm raising him or her." I told her that because if the nigga thought Maylan was pregnant by him, he'd show his face; especially when he said he did it on purpose.

"Why couldn't you love me Vernon?" This bitch had the nerve to pull out a small .22 and point it at me. Dante and I both shook our heads.

"Oh you're going to shoot me?" She walked out the bathroom.

"No, I'm going to kill that bitch the minute you leave her side." She took off running. I tried to catch her but because she was half way down the hall when she said it, she had a head start.

"I see the old Vernon is going to have to show his face."

"Lets hope not." I heard and detective Will came closer to me. He shook my hand and sat me down in the waiting room. He told us about this Jared guy and it was pretty much the same from the file Birch brought me last night. The thing that stuck out was he preyed on women like Maylan. He wanted a family and if the woman didn't give it to him, he'd kill them. There are a few missing women he had been with but with no body they couldn't charge him. The reason he was charged with the last one was because her family sent the cops to the house after they couldn't reach her for days. He had scratches on his face or some shit and they used self-defense.

"But why Maylan?" I asked with my head back staring at the ceiling.

"I don't think he picked her out but when he came up for Abel, she was who he chose. He goes after woman who has no family and appears to be weak in his eyes. Maylan may not have been weak to you but others see different; plus its no telling what Abel told him." I nodded.

"I'm going to have two of my best men guarding her room. I know you won't leave but these guys have served in the military and they won't be dressed in police clothes. I want them to appear normal as possible in case he does try and come up here or that crazy bitch who just left." I jumped up and ran in the room when I heard them over the intercom ask for a doctor on the ICU floor. We got in there and Isa was crying.

"Her water broke and... Man its too early." Birch was panicking, which made everyone else do the same. Maylan's machine started beeping. We all turned to look and her eyes were fluttering. I ran and picked her hand up.

"Baby, I'm right here." I kissed her lips.

"We have to clear this room out." Isa screamed real loud and you saw blood coming down her leg in the wheelchair. What the fuck was going on? They wheeled her out fast and the nurses pushed me out the room and closed the door.

"Vernon she's going to be fine." My mom said rubbing my back.

"I can't take this shit." I yelled out and made my way to the elevator. The detective was behind me and so were Smitty and Barry.

"Bro you can't leave." Barry said.

"Mannnn. I'm not about to sit here and let them tell me she died. Nah, I gotta go." I stepped on the elevator.

"VERNON! VERNON!" They all shouted as the doors closed. I made my way to the car and sped out the parking lot to go see my son. Right now I needed some peace and he was the only one who could give it to me.

Mike opened the door holding VJ and told me to hit the shower. I glanced down at myself and I still had Maylan's blood on me. I stripped and took a long shower. I put my basketball shorts on with a wife beater and found Mike and my son on the couch.

"Thanks Mike." I took VJ from him who was sucking on his pacifier looking around. I told him to turn on cartoons because he seemed to like it.

"I don't think she's going to make it." I said out the blue and laid on the couch.

"Son, you can't think like that. Look, God hasn't taken her for a reason. Yes, the machines wee going off but it could've been because she heard you and is trying to find her way back. Maylan knows you love her and she's not about to leave you or VJ." I wiped my eyes. I felt like a chick with all the crying I did, but damn Maylan was my heart and it broke me to see her like that. I didn't ask how he knew about the machines. I'm sure my mom called before I got here.

81

"You have to find your way back to the hospital so you can be there when she wakes up. I know it's hard and I can't imagine what you're going through but I do know she'd want you there. Get you some sleep and go back up there tomorrow. I'm going up there to sit with my wife. She isn't doing too well seeing her like that either."

"Thanks. Tell her I'll be up there first thing."

"Vernon make sure you come. You don't want Maylan to think you turned your back on her." I nodded and locked up after he left. Me and my son ate and went to bed. I tossed and turned all night, while my son slept with no problems. I stared at him and even though he had all my looks, I could see a little of his mom in there. I said a silent prayer to God that he lets her make it.

Abel

"Are you ok?" Lique asked me for the millionth time since she's been here. At first I stayed in her new condo with her after Dante almost killed me when he ran me off the road but Birch came there when I was in the shower and she got nervous.

"I'm good Lique. How's my baby?" I rubbed her stomach. She had two more months left and a nigga couldn't wait. Yea, I have kids but it's been a while since I've been around a newborn.

"Fine. I'm ready to have her already." She climbed in the bed next to me. We found out she was having a girl when she turned five months. I looked down at her lying on my chest and actually thought about making an honest woman out of her. Its just I can't help but to think about how she doesn't have her son as much and being Isa isn't coming back, I may as well have someone to grow old with. Lique has good pussy, great head, cooks, cleans and caters to me like a king.

"Go take a shower. I'm going to take you out to eat."

"Really." She got excited like we've never been out."

"Yea, I'm hungry and I know my daughter is." She had a big grin on her face. I know she gets a kick out of me being nice to her. She explained how Birch never made it official with her but people knew not to mess with her. I guess she felt like he was ashamed but it was far from the truth. He may not have told her they were a couple but every nigga out here knew she was his. A man doesn't have to say we're boyfriend or girlfriend because what's understood doesn't have to be explained.

I heard someone knocking on the door and went down the steps to get it. I wasn't worried about anyone coming to my spot because only a few people knew of this place; including this nigga.

"What up?" I said to Jared who came in disheveled like a motherfucker.

"Yo, I got to get the fuck out of town." He paced back and forth as I closed the door. I stood there waiting for him to explain why.

The purpose of him coming here was to help me in the apartment complexes we were going to take over. After Isa got arrested, he went after Maylan more aggressively to get her to go back into the apartment so we could get back to business. Unfortunately, the apartment was emptied and rented to someone else. Now I got them handling business out of Lique's condo but she doesn't know because we are extra careful. I don't want to take another loss; plus Lique is pregnant.

I continued listening to him ramble on and still had no idea what he was saying. All I heard was Maylan and that nigga Vernon is coming for him. Why did these niggas insist on fucking with his crazy ass, is beyond me?

"Yo, calm the fuck down and tell me what happened from the beginning." I handed him a beer and sat there listening to him tell me how he tried to kill Maylan and would have succeeded if Vernon and his boys didn't show up.

"Hold up. You tried to kill her on purpose? What the fuck yo?" I asked with my face turned up. Maylan cool as hell and I'm not sure what he wanted to do that for.

"Man fuck that bitch. She was having secret meetings with her ex. I think she was fucking him and you know I don't share."

"Weren't you fucking Celeste?" I knew that because Lique told me.

"Come on Abel. You know how we get down. I can have all the pussy I want, but my main bitch ain't got no business with another nigga."

"They got a kid together bro." He waved me off.

"Listen, You got to get out of town. If he found her and you claim she's basically dead, he's going to come for you and I can guarantee he will not stop take it easy on you."

"I ain't worried about no cornball ass nigga. I'm leaving because I'm not trying to go to jail." People slept on those SFN niggas all the time but little did they know, they were just as street as us. I chuckled at the thought of the chicks calling them that back in the day.

"Jail? Vernon ain't no snitch and I doubt he even lets you make it there once he finds you."

That's when I remembered he did the same shit to another woman in Virginia but he beat the case. I couldn't believe he came here pulling the same shit. Luckily, he doesn't know too much about my operation, otherwise I could see him trying to hang shit over my head to help him. I'm not getting in the middle of this disaster he created. I wanted to contact Isa. I know she is going crazy right now.

After talking to him, I went upstairs and saw Lique on the bed looking teary eyed.

"What's the matter?"

"Did he kill her?"

84

"I don't know Lique. The way he described what he did to her; I'm not sure if she survived." I heard arguing downstairs where I left him and it was Celeste and him arguing over something. I put my finger to my lips to tell her to stay quiet and turned the television down.

"Is she dead?" I heard him ask Celeste.

"No, but she's pregnant."

"She is?" He asked with excitement in his voice.

"Yea and he said he's raising the baby."

"No the fuck he's not. I purposely got her pregnant and I'll be damned if another man raises it. I have to see her."

"You can't get anywhere near her."

"What you mean?"

"I mean her room is on lockdown. Vernon, his boys, their women, and parents aren't allowing anyone in. If you want to speak to her you're going to have to wait until she wakes up and you catch her outside."

"Nah. I'm going to get in there to see her."

"Why are you obsessing over her."

"Bitch, ain't nobody obsessing over her but if that's my kid, I have to play nice until she has the baby and then I'm out. You knew the plan was to have a kid with her and disappear so you can get your man back. Why you acting like you don't know what it is?" Did these two dummies concoct this dumb plan together? No wonder it isn't working out for them. I took Lique hand and walked down the steps with her.

"You know you're sexy as hell in this dress." I whispered in her ear on the way to where dumb and dumber was.

"Its all for you baby." I yanked her back gently and pushed her in the bathroom. I lifted her dress and pushed inside her.

"Shitttt Abel. Mmmmm." She moaned out and bit down on her bottom lip. I stroked in and out slow and stared at her eyes roll in the back of her head.

"You my woman Lique?" Her eyes popped open.

"If you want me to be."

"Nah, the question is, are you my woman?" I went deep and she grabbed the back of my neck.

"Yes baby, yesssss."

"You love me."

"I love you so much Abel. Fuckkkk."

"I love you too Lique and that's on some real shit."

85

"You do." I went faster and watching her cream coat my dick, made me cum fast.

"I do Lique. I'm not going to say I'm in love with you but I can feel it coming eventually. You are a good woman but you have to work on spending more time with your son and being a better mom to him."

"I want to Abel but Birch won't allow me to." She began cleaning both of us off. I lifted her chin.

"That's your fault."

"I know and I'm going to do better. I don't need you fighting with him either."

"You do know we're going to get into it again after what went down at his house and him going in the hospital."

"After y'all get that fight out your system, then that's it. My son was devastated seeing his dad in there and my daughter needs to have her father around too." I nodded my head.

"Let's go. I'm hungry and I know your horny ass is going to want more dick when we get back." She laughed. I smacked her on the ass and followed her in the room with those two still arguing.

"Alright y'all. We about to bounce." Celeste stared Lique up and down with a smirk on her face. This had to be the most jealous woman I've ever known. The doorbell rang and I opened it to see Kacey on the other side of it.

"Who the fuck called you here and what happened to you?" She stepped inside and spoke to everyone. She had a slight limp and her face was fucked up.

"Dante." I put my hand up.

"I told you to leave that nigga and his family alone and now look. He beat the shit out of you and if you're here, it means he's looking for you." She sucked her teeth and started going up the stairs.

"Ugh, where you going?"

"To the bedroom. I'm tired Abel and-"

"There is no more bedroom for you here. Remember you moved out in hopes Dante would want you. Take your ass home Kacey."

"Abel, why can't I?"

"You should've stayed your ass home and I'm on my way out."

"Ok. I'll be here when you get back."

"Kacey, my girl don't want you here. You gotta go." I saw Lique stare at me. She isn't scared of Kacey but she's pregnant and Kacey is one of those bitches who don't care and will still fight you."

86

"Awww shit now." Jared said and took a seat. Celeste had the nerve to sit on his lap.

"Your girl! When the hell did you get a woman?"

"That's none of your business but she's about to have my daughter and you staying here is not an option."

"You're having another baby."

"Go head with that Kacey. You sat here and told me you wanted Dante and planned on getting pregnant. What, you thought I would sit around waiting for you to figure it out."

"Who is she?" I saw Celeste sneaky ass point to Lique and Kacey took off to get her. I jumped in front of Lique and told her not to say anything. I don't need them arguing and she get stressed out. Kacey started yelling about how she could do that to her and they were friends. Jared was laughing and so was Celeste, which I couldn't wait to bust her bubble.

"Lique was never your friend. You met her through Celeste so stop trying to get at her. Celeste however, was your best friend and I fucked her plenty of times. Ain't that right Celeste?" Her mouth fell open and she didn't get a chance to defend herself as Kacey rocked the shit out of her. I let them go at if for a few minutes until Lique said she was ready to go.

"Alright y'all gots to go. My girl is hungry." I lifted Kacey off Celeste and Jared grabbed Celeste to leave.

"Abel why would you tell her? I thought we said it would be a secret."

"Celeste you are one jealous bitch who wants every body else's man instead of getting your own. Did you ever think that none of the men you were with left their main chick for you? Before you say it, the only reason Vernon got back with you after Maylan, was on some accident type shit. Jared doesn't even want you and using your stupid ass for information. You have to be the dumbest bitch I know. Get the fuck out." Jared shook his head laughing and Kacey stood there staring at Lique.

"Yo, if you even think about laying hands on her, I'm fucking you up."

"Abel."

"She was not your friend Kacey, so stop. You were friends through that other dumb bitch and it's been plenty of times you called her all types of names for shit you said she did. Lique don't owe you shit but Celeste who claimed to be both of y'all best friend, is the one

87

who you need to go for and since you did, its over. Now like I said my girl is hungry." I opened the door for her.

"But-"

"Bye Kacey and if she tells me you got at her in any way, I'm coming for you."

"What about your son?" I yoked her up.

"Bitch, I have never neglected my kids and I'm not about to start. Don't even think about using him against me because I'll take him."

"I wouldn't do that Abel."

"Then don't bring shit about him up." I pushed her out the door and slammed it in her face.

"You ok?"

"Yea. But I'm still hungry for food and this." She grabbed my dick.

"Which one you want first because you can have whatever you want." I licked my lips and hoped it was dick.

"I think your man wants me to taste him first. What you think? She asked kissing me and unzipping my jeans. Needless to say we never went out that night and ordered take out.

Isa

After I saw Maylan in the ICU, I began to think about all the times she wanted to talk to me. Birch, told me to speak to her and find out what was going on and I planned on doing it but she never came in the house. I called her over and over but she refused to answer. I called Birch and asked him to get Vernon to call but she wouldn't answer for him either. Maylan had a lot of shit going on and I shouldn't have left her out in the cold but she did it to me. It's not right to be tit for tat and that's not what I tried to do. I wanted her to realize that the world doesn't revolve around her and I had kids to look out for.

Now I'm sitting on the maternity floor staring at my daughter Ariel lying on her fathers' chest. I went into early labor and delivered her through a C-section a few days ago. My pressure was still high so they kept me longer. Ariel had her lungs checked and because she was over five pounds she was good to go home when I did. Birch refused to let her out of his sight and argued with everyone who wanted to hold her. Him and his mom actually got into a big argument over it. She left and said she wasn't coming back up until he left because she was going to choke him. Katarina and Brayden loved Ariel and already made plans on who would hold her first when she came home.

Maylan's mom called to say her and her husband were out of rehab and looking for her. They wanted to meet their grandbaby but Vernon wouldn't allow it. I think he was still pissed over her not telling him how she was the day she got shot. Birch told me she came up to the hospital and Vernon almost cursed her out for trying to call the shots on what she wanted to doctors to do. He said her father just sat there with his head on Maylan's arm and kept apologizing for not being a better man for her.

Vernon's mom had to jump in because Maylan's mom tried to hit him and well that was not happening. I wish I saw it so I could tell her when she woke up.

"You good over there?" Birch asked.

"Yea, I'm just thinking about Maylan. I'm going to take a shower and I want to see her." He said ok and put the baby in the crib to help me in the bathroom. It hurt to walk but knowing I had active kids at home, I would have to deal with it.

"Stop licking your lips Birch because you're not getting any." I told him and went to open the bathroom door.

"You sure." He sat on the top of the toilet stroking himself.

"Why you playing?" Now it was my turn to lick my lips. Birch knew I loved giving him head. I guess I could give him something to hold him over. I grabbed his hand and had him stand and took over stroking it. I sat on the toilet and pulled him close.

"Damn baby." His hand was on my head. I grabbed the back of his ass to push him in to go farther.

"Fuckkkk Isa." My fingers were under his balls juggling them at the same time I jerked him with the other one. I let spit fall on the tip and my tongue slid in and out of it. His knees were shaking and he tried to push me away. When he got like this, it meant he was about to cum hard and he would always moan.

"Give it to me Brayden." I stared up at him and he was looking down at me biting his lip hard as hell. He pumped faster in my mouth.

"Got dammit Isaaaaaa. Shittttt." His sperm shot down my throat. I recycled it in my mouth an on his dick a few times. He loved when I did this.

"Yea Brayden. Mmmmm you taste good." He lifted me up and his kiss was aggressive but warranted. I wanted him in the worse way but it was no way possible. He couldn't even go down on me.

"I fucking love you woman." He yanked my head back and attacked my neck as his hands caressed my breasts.

"Sssss we have to stop." He wasn't listening. I had to push him away.

"Damn I want you so bad right now Isa."

"I want you too baby." His man was hard again so I gave him one of my infamous hand jobs and he was satisfied, for now. I cleaned my mouth out, washed up and he got himself together as well. We walked out the bathroom and Ariel was asleep and the door was still shut. I sat in the chair as he removed the sheets off the bed and tossed them on the floor. I always asked for clean sheets whenever I cleaned up. He went outside and asked the nurse to have housekeeping come in and put down new ones.

"Your mom is on her way to watch Ariel so we can go see Maylan."

"I could've stayed in here with her."

"Birch, Ariel is her granddaughter and you're being a bully when it comes to her."

"So, she's my daughter."

"Birch stop it. Vernon is probably there too and I'm sure he needs a break. Take him out or something."

"I guess."

"Awww come here baby." I kissed his lips.

"Ariel lives with us and you'll be around her way more than everyone else. Let your mom enjoy her moment too. Now she'll be here soon so fix your face."

"Why do you need his mom when yours is here?" I lifted my head and my mom came in holding balloons and flowers. Birch looked at me and could tell how pissed I was. He asked me a few times if I was ok but I ignored him and stared at my mother.

"What the fuck are you doing here?"

"ISA!" Birch yelled out.

"Not right now babe. What the fuck you want?" I asked and in walked the nigga she kicked me out for, licking his lips.

"Yo, motherfucker is something wrong with your mouth?" He ignored Birch and my mom came closer to me.

"Back up." I stood up and Birch stood in front of me.

"Isa, why are you acting like that?"

"You know why but since you want me to say it, I'll tell you." I stepped around him and got in her face.

"Never mind." She said.

"No you wanted to know, so I'm going to say it." I watched her try and leave and grabbed her arm.

"How dare you come up here after you tossed me and my kids on the street? I know I was grown at the time but my babies didn't deserve to be homeless."

"Well that nigga should've taken care of you." She was speaking of Abel.

"Ok but he didn't and when I came to you on those cold nights with my babies and you wouldn't open your door, you showed me who you really were."

"Isa you slept with my man."

"Are you sure about that?" I asked and folded my arms. She didn't respond.

"Exactly. Yes, he was attracted to me and I can tell his nasty ass still is but I would never sleep with my moms' boyfriend. You were my mother and when I came to tell you the way he was acting around me, it was your responsibility to handle him, not throw me out."

"But the times I came home and heard you moaning."

91

"I had my own man at the time and you should've known that because I had a kid by him and one on the way. You saw Abel at the house all the time and he paid you money to stay there when he didn't want to leave at night. I didn't see you complaining then. It wasn't until he left me that you thought something else was going on. You chose a man over your own daughter and I will never forgive you for that."

"Isa I thought-"

"I don't care what you thought. I was your daughter. I was the one with kids who lived in a fucking shed for a year. Not one time did you offer me help. My kids don't know you and never will."

"Isa I'm trying to make it right."

"How can you make it right when you're with the same man you kicked me out for? Baby, can you make them leave?" I looked at Birch and he walked past me to my mom.

"Nigga, I ain't going anywhere." She said.

"Look, I'm not sure what happened between the two of you but that's my fiancé and if she wants you out, then you got to go. I don't put my hands on women but if you push me one more time, I'm going to knock you the fuck out." My mom must've seen the seriousness in his face because she backed up.

"Who is this?" I heard his mom come in talking.

"Isa, don't do this." I heard my mom scream out.

"Lets go baby. Fuck that bitch." I heard her boyfriend say and then I heard a loud thud. I looked and he was on the ground knocked out.

"Oh my God."

"Welp! I told y'all to leave. Don't bring your ass around my woman or kids again."

"Those are my grandkids."

"Too bad." Birch closed the door in her face.

"You good." I nodded my head yes and sat down. I stayed in that chair for about an hour. My mother called security and tried to have them arrest Birch for knocking her boyfriend out. They said it wasn't happening since he asked them to leave a lot of times and she kept pushing him. Birch knew the guy anyway so my mom had no win, whatsoever. I told Birch I was ready to see Maylan. I had to get out the room for a while. His moms' boyfriend came up and the two of them acted like they needed private time of their own.

"How is she?" I asked Vernon who was lying in the bed with her.

"Her eyes are still black and blue but they're not swollen. The dentist came in today and said they're going to fix her teeth early next week. Its better for them to try and get in to do it while she's still here."

"What are they going to do?"

"They don't know if they're going to do dentures or try and replace the ones missing. When they get in her mouth they'll know."

"How did you get a dentist to come here?"

"Money talks Isa."

"Ok. What about the wounds and her arm?"

"Her arm will be fine once the cast is removed, the wounds are healing and the antibiotics for the disease he gave her, is going to keep them from being infected. I know she hears us talking because her fingers move once in a while. She is trying to come back but I'm not sure if I'm ready for her to wake up."

"Why?"

"Because her body is most likely still in a lot of pain and I don't want that for her. It may sound selfish but I'd rather her be healed and able to walk right out of here when she wakes up, then to wake up and have to struggle." I saw his hand was holding hers.

"Lets take a walk." Birch said. At first he wasn't willing but the two guards outside at the nurses station dressed as techs came in when he nodded. He told them I'd be there and they are to keep a close eye on us. Once he felt comfortable they left the room.

I stayed in the room for a few hours. Birch called to tell me he took Vernon to the room to meet Ariel who he hadn't seen because he wouldn't leave May. Then he took him home to change and get something to eat. I sat there talking to Maylan knowing she couldn't respond. I think her finger moved when I mentioned what went down in my room when my mom came. I didn't hate my mom and I forgave her a long time ago but she didn't have to right to inquire about me or my kids when she is still with the same guy she accused me of sleeping with.

My mom knew Abel and I were together and told him he could stay with us. I'm sure it was because he gave her money for the bills and food. I cooked, cleaned and took damn good care of my kids. Yea, I shouldn't have been having sex in my moms' house but she was barely ever there because of the boyfriend.

Unfortunately, he lost his job and she moved him in with us. At the same time Abel was distancing himself away from me. He no

93

longer gave me money for the kids and would come by at night and only have sex with me or ask me to go down on him. I don't know if he ever truly loved me but I got my two babies out of him.

The night my mom assumed I was with her man, I was in my room pleasing myself. I had no idea she even heard me because she was supposed to be at work. The next day I got out of bed and she was sitting on the couch smoking a cigarette and told me to get my kids shit and leave. I asked her what happened and she said I had sex with her man. I cried and begged her to stay but she didn't want to hear it.

I had nowhere to go and went to Maylan's. I stayed at her house for a few days but her mom kept saying Maylan had to prepare herself for the guys coming to buy her. I used to think she was lying about that but when her mom asked me was I going to do the same thing, I knew it was time to go.

I tried calling Abel but each time he said I needed to have sex with him and I was over that. I never told him we were homeless but if I did and he got me a place, I'd really be stuck with him and I needed to move forward. One day Maylan and I were walking and saw the shed. It wasn't much but we got our stuff from her moms' house and made that our home. We got a job and the rest is history.

"Hey Isa. I'm so glad you're here." Maylan's mom came in hugging me and her father went to the other side of the bed.

"I've been here but I had my daughter."

"I heard. A girl right." I shook my head yes.

"Maylan is going to be excited to hear that." I smiled because she wanted me to have another girl.

"I'm having her moved." Her mom said and I stared at her.

"What? Vernon is not going for that."

"Fuck Vernon. He is the reason Maylan has endured so much pain." I sent Birch a text and told him he needed Vernon to get up here fast. I loved Maylan's mom but she was about to cause unnecessary drama.

"He loves her."

"Yea right."

"They're married and she wouldn't be happy if you did this."

"You say he loves her but this isn't the first time she's been here because of him." She completely ignored me saying they were married. I guess if she didn't witness it, she didn't believe it.

94

"That's for Maylan to deal with. He is in love with her and hasn't left her side. The only reason he's not here right now is because my fiancé took him out to get air."

"If he loved her, she wouldn't be going through this." She ran her hand down Maylan's face.

"If you loved her, she would've never run away from you trying to sell her. If you loved her, you wouldn't be trying to dictate her love life knowing she can't defend herself. If you loved her, it wouldn't have taken you all those years to get off drugs. Do I need to go on?" Vernon said standing there staring her down. Her father gave Vernon a handshake.

"Who are you to judge me when your ex is the one who caused all this bullshit. You were supposed to protect her but here she is again." She pointed to Maylan.

"She's not here because of me this time. Maylan made a decision for herself and left me alone. This has nothing to do with me but you damn right I'm here. Now if you're only here to talk shit, you can bounce." He moved away and got on the bed with her.

"I got something better." She left and came in the room ten minutes later with a couple of cops. Vernon started laughing.

"Sir, we have to ask you to leave." One of the officers said.

"For what?"

"She said this is her daughter and you're not welcomed here."

"And she's my wife so you can tell her, she can leave."

"He's lying." Vernon lifted Maylan's hand with a wedding band on her finger and reached in his pocket. I don't even know when he put the ring on her finger. It may have been there and I wasn't paying it no mind.

"Prove it." He handed the cops a piece of paper that said marriage license on it. I thought Maylan ripped it up but he must've went and got another one.

"This is bullshit." She ripped it up and Vernon got pissed.

"Yo, get her out of here." They escorted her out screaming and cursing. I asked Birch to take me back to the room. I couldn't take anymore of the bullshit today.

"I'm ready to go home." I told him as he laid down next to me. Ariel was asleep on my chest and of course he took her. She was going to be spoiled as hell and no one is going to be able to handle her but him.

"Its too late now, but I'll make sure the doctor discharges you tomorrow." He kissed my forehead and we fell asleep together.

Maylan

"Baby, I need you to wake up." I heard him and couldn't figure out how he got here. The entire time I was asleep, I could hear Vernon saying no one is allowed in here unless its family so how did he get in. I was trying so hard to fight and open my eyes but right now, I was fighting to keep them closed.

"Hurry up. Vernon only went downstairs and the two cops are going to come back soon." I heard the voice of the woman who said she was his cousin. I felt his lips touch the top of my lips and he rubbed on my stomach for some reason.

"I love you Maylan." If I could laugh I would've. How is he claiming he loved me after all the shit he put me through. A few minutes later I heard Vernon come in the room and he had to be on the phone because I didn't hear anyone responding to him.

"I gotta go." I heard him say.

"Open those eyes for me Maylan. Please baby." I felt him kissing my hand.

"You're almost there May. Come on, you can do it." I loved hearing him call my nickname. I opened my eyes and closed them back.

"Hold on. Let me shut the light off." He dropped my hand and picked it back up a few seconds later. I opened my eyes again and he had tears coming down his face. I tried to speak but the thing in my mouth wouldn't let me. I went to pull it out but my arm had a cast on it and he stopped me. I heard him tell the nurse to get a doctor in here to check me because I'm awake.

After the doctor came in along with two nurses, he did an exam. He checked my eyes, reflexes and a bunch of other shit. The nurse took my vitals and he was sending me down to x-ray to check my chest. The second she stepped out the room Vernon hugged me tight and wouldn't let go. I heard him crying more and tried to wipe his eyes but he had a tight grip on me. He looked up at me and wiped my tears before kissing me.

Something was weird about my mouth. I put my hand up to touch it and he explained how I had to get dentures on the top of my teeth and they replaced the ones at the bottom and capped a few.

"Maylan, you're good. Don't worry about none of that. You still look beautiful to me and that's all that matters." I shook my head and let him carry me in the bathroom. I didn't have to tell him I wanted to be cleaned. He knew how I was, started the shower and sat me on the chair inside. I had small bandages over my chest and they were getting wet so he pulled the nurse button.

"Is everything ok?" Shit, they come faster if you pull the one in the bathroom.

"Her bandages are getting wet. Can we get some new ones and can you ask house keeping to change her sheets?" The nurse told him yes and if I wasn't mistaken flirted a little.

"She wants you Vernon." I told him as he removed the showerhead and washed the soap off.

"I don't want anyone but you May." He kissed me again and this time his tongue slipped in. It felt weird with these damn teeth but I have to get used to them.

"Vernon, I'm sorry for everything. I was so angry with you and Celeste and he was supposed to be a distraction but he hurt me. I want you to know that I never stopped loving you."

"May, none of that matters now. You're awake babe and I hope you know you're coming home with me."

"Vernon, you still want me?" He lifted my chin.

"I will always want you Maylan. I love you. You are my son's mother and my wife." I covered my mouth.

"What's wrong?"

"I ripped the paper up and it was never redone."

"Do you still want to be my wife? I know I say you are but is it what you want?" I nodded my head yes and kissed him feverishly to let him know I meant it.

"Then I'm calling the reverend and this time you're signing it before he walks out the room." He wrapped the towel around me and stood me up to step out and get dressed. All I could put on was a gown but his mom was bringing me stuff. He called her before he started the shower to tell her I was awake. Housekeeping was finishing up with the bed as we came out and the chick who saved me from Jared the one day was sitting there texting on her phone.

"Why are you here?"

"Maylan she's been here waiting for you to wake up. I thought she helped you the first day you two met.

"She's keeping tabs on my progress for him Vernon." I started crying because if she was here, it meant he knew I was awake and there's no telling if he'd come back to finish the job.

98

"WHAT?" Vernon had her yanked up by the throat.

"I left you in here with her thinking she was safe and you were here for him. I should kill you."

"Yo, what the fuck you doing to my wife." Dave came in and pushed Vernon away from her. She was on the ground gasping for air.

"Dave, she let him in here. He was here before Vernon came back."

"WHAT? That nigga in the hospital?" Vernon was fuming.

"Babe, I know you weren't on no grimy shit with him. I know he's your cousin but you saw what he did to her. Yo, my man, I apologize for her actions. I didn't know she did that."

"He said she was pregnant by him and he wanted to help her. I'm sorry Maylan." She was crying staring at me.

"Get her the fuck out of here and she better not come back." Dave snatched her up.

"Wait!" I yelled out as loud as I could.

"Did you tell him I'm awake?" We all looked at her.

"I'm sorry Maylan but he knows." Her husband was more pissed than Vernon.

"Baby, you have to get me out of here. He's going to come back. Please get me out of here." I tried to walk but it was hard being I've been in bed for so long.

"Maylan, I swear on our son he will not get to you again. I'm not leaving your side and you can believe if I do need to step out, one of my boys will be here."

"I still want to leave Vernon. Please."

"Ok. Ok. Let me get the doctor to come in and see if we can get you discharged and have someone come check on you there."

"Wait! Where are you going?" I asked when he opened the door.

"To the desk. I can see you May." He pointed to the window and he was right the desk was maybe fifty feet away. I stared at him speak to the doctor and come back to the room. I moved over in the bed and he got in with me. I moved so close to him he had to tell me to relax because I was about to push him out the bed.

An hour later the reverend came in and so did Birch, Isa and everyone else. The room was crowded as we did our little ceremony and like Vernon said, he made me sign the paper before he left. Vernon asked everyone to step out so Isa and I could talk. She stood up and gave me a hug and we stayed in that position for a good five minutes crying. We moved back from one another and wiped our eyes.

"I'm sorry for not listening to you all the times you came to see me. If I had, I would've known something was wrong and."

"Isa, I made all my decisions on my own. I left you hanging for some of the most important things in your life and I am so sorry. You have always been the strong one out of us and I assumed nothing I did bothered you. I missed you so much."

"I missed you too and you have a niece named Ariel now."

"I heard she's beautiful." Isa gave me a look.

"Vernon said he wants a daughter now." She started laughing.

"Yea, and had I not had a c section, Birch would've put another one in me already."

"Let me find out we got these niggas strung off some homeless pussy." We both fell out. We used to always say one of us would throw our homeless pussy on a nigga with money and get us out the shed. Well, we both did it and it worked. She started telling me how my mom came in here bugging and her mom did the same. I heard when she told me before but I thought I was dreaming.

We sat in there for a good hour talking about everything before Vernon came in and said the doctor was discharging me and we would stop by later. Isa kissed me and gave Vernon a hug, which shocked the hell out of me.

"When did you two become friends?" I asked once everyone left. He told me at the hospital when Birch got hurt. I guess its true when they say a tragedy brings people together.

We got the discharge papers and left the hospital. I found myself being paranoid but he yelled at me. I had no doubt in my mind he would protect me but how can I protect him? I may not be a fighter but I'm not going to allow anyone to hit on him either.

He parked in front of his moms' and carried me in the house. Vernon would not allow me to walk for some reason. The doctor said to take my time but damn. He brought my son to me and I broke down crying. A month in the hospital is a long time to be away from the people who loved you. My son had his hand on my lip playing with them as he sucked on the pacifier. I asked Vernon if we could stay the night because I was tired and didn't feel like going back out. He told me yes and took VJ to get a bath and ready for bed.

"You ready for bed?" His mom and Mike had gone upstairs hours ago.

"Yes but let me walk." He helped me up and once we got to the steps I had him carry me. It was too many stairs and I only walked once today to use the bathroom and he had to carry me back.

"Is my wife comfortable?"

"Yup. Is my husband?"

"Never been better." He kissed my lips and had me lay on his chest. I missed everything about him and its nice to know he felt the same.

Vernon

Maylan has been out the hospital for two weeks and she was horny as hell and wanted the D but I couldn't do her like that. Its not like I didn't want it but none of us told her Jared gave her those diseases nor did I get my own results back from the clinic. She was clean as far as the STD's went and the HIV test was negative.

I never slept with Celeste unprotected which let me know in order to be pregnant, she most likely poked holes in the condom and if she had anything to do with the same guy, I'm sure she fucked him too. I didn't think about going to the clinic because I didn't feel like anything was wrong but my mom told me to go. They called me today and asked me to come to the office and a nigga was sick. I could've gotten the results sooner if it was just for the STD's but I took a HIV test too and everyone gets nervous waiting on those results.

"Hi Mr. Davis. Can you follow me to the back?" The nurse asked and placed me in a room. I looked down at my phone and opened up the photo message and it was Maylan naked in the tub with bubbles covering her body. I closed it real fast because my man started to wake up.

"Hello Mr. Davis. I see you're here for the result of your blood work."

"Yup. Give it to me straight. Am I going to die?" he laughed.

"No Mr. Davis you're not going to die. All your tests came back negative."

"Why did I have to come down here to get the results?"

"Sir, that information is confidential and anyone can call pretending they're you. What if you did have something and the other person told everyone. We have to protect your confidentiality."

"Ok cool." I grabbed my results out his hand and headed to my house but stopped at this store to get her some chocolate covered strawberries. She loves those damn things. I asked my mom to keep VJ for the night and I would pick him up tomorrow. When she asked me why, I told her because I'm about to get Maylan pregnant again. She hung up on me for some reason. I stopped by Birch's house to see the kids and headed home around eight. I wasn't worried about Maylan because no one knew where she was and it's going to stay like that.

"May." I yelled out when I got home but she didn't answer. I ain't going to lie, I started to get nervous. I locked the door and searched upstairs and she wasn't there. I ran back down the steps and heard low music coming from the kitchen.

When I walked in she was pouring caramel syrup, which is my favorite, down her body. I dropped the strawberries on the table and watched her grind her body on the kitchen island as the liquid slid down her nipples, to her stomach and in her middle. I licked my lips watching her place two fingers inside and moan out. I undid the button and zipper to my jeans and let them hit the floor. I came out of my boxers and t-shirt and tossed them. I moved closer to her and kissed her in a sensual rhythm that made us hotter than we were.

"I missed you baby." She whispered and brought her fingers up to my mouth. I sucked her juices and the caramel off and placed my fingers inside. She was trying to calm herself but her breaths were increasing rapidly and her orgasm was coming fast.

"Suck my pussy Vernon. I want you to make me cum with your mouth." I pulled one of the bar stools over, sat on it and spread her legs apart as if I were a gynecologist. The only light on was over the stove but it was just enough to see her pussy glistening as she waited for my mouth to make its way down. I allowed her mound to grow as I sucked over and over. I intensely stroked her clit and watched the way her body arched as she began to convulse.

"Cum for me May." I allowed my tongue to do circles on her clitoris and within seconds she fed me her sweet nectar that I could never get enough of. I continued stroking her with my fingers and slurping up her juices as more escaped her body with each release.

"Gawdddddd, I love you so much Vernon." She sat up, lifted my head and leaned down for a kiss. I licked the caramel off her toes, her legs, stomach and breasts as she moaned out in delight. I was ready to enter her but she pushed me back and stepped away to grab something.

"Oh shit what's that?" I asked when I felt something hot all over but it wasn't like fire.

"Its called ginger honey heat. Do you like it?" She asked making circles with it on my body and then stopping.

"Yea May. It feels good. Shitttttt." Her lips wrapped around my dick and I threw my head back on the wall. She pulled her mouth back and her tongue ran inside the slit of the tip, and then sucked the head like a blow pop. She lifted my dick and sucked my balls whole in her mouth. I was losing control and my knees were shaking. My wife was doing the damn thing with her mouth. I heard her spit and felt both of her hands jerking me off at the same time as she sucked the tip.

"How's this Vernon?" It was dark but I could feel her eyes on mine and I'm sure she felt the same. I felt her cheeks going in and out as she suctioned my dick like a vacuum.

"May, I can't hold it anymore. Arghhhhhh."

"Mmmmm. Yea baby. Give it all to me. Mmmmm." She said and continued sucking. By the time she finished I was ready for bed. I fell in one of the chairs out of breath and felt her climb on top of me.

"I don't want you to make love to me tonight baby. I need you to fuck me and take out all your anger on me for leaving you." She sucked on my neck and used her hand to rub my dick on her pussy that was soaked.

"You sure?"

"Positive baby." Once I got hard, she slid down and I let her fuck the hell out of me in that chair. I knew she wouldn't be able to function when I finished.

"Yea May, make me cum again." I felt her muscles squeezing my dick and not too long after I came inside her womb and prayed she got pregnant again. I lifted her up and carried her upstairs. There's no way she'll be able to move when I'm done so we may as well be up here.

"Vernon don't leave me."

"Never baby. You stuck for life." I rammed myself in her and she screamed out instantly. This is what she wanted and unless she begged me to stop, I'm giving it to her. I placed her legs back like she was a baby and had her hold her cheeks open at the same time. I dug so deep a nigga got scared when she stopped moaning. I looked at her and she had her eyes rolling in the back of her head. I dropped her legs and flipped her over.

"Vernon I'm cumming againnnnnnnnn." Her juices spit on my stomach.

"That's right May. Show me how much you missed me fucking you." She threw her ass back and that was it. We went at it like damn porn stars. By the time we finished it was damn near two in the morning.

"I have never had any pussy this fucking good." I laid back on the bed with her on top of me.

"Homeless pussy is good huh?"

104

"Yo, don't say that shit May. You're not homeless." I tried to push her off but we were still sticky and she wouldn't let me.

"I know Vernon. It's a joke Isa and I used to say when we were." She told me some dumb story and I told her don't say it again.

"I want to get in the shower but I can't move."

"Then don't. You're my wife and I know you're not dirty."

"Yea, but we're going to regret it." I rolled her off me and she laid there.

"Come on May or I'm getting back in the bed."

"Carry me daddy." I had to smile when she said it. I carried her in the bathroom like she asked.

"I missed you Maylan." I kissed her shoulder and washed her up. I've been catering to her everyday since she's been home.

"I missed you too Vernon and I can't say it enough about how sorry I am." She wrapped her arms around my neck. We kissed for a few minutes and I finished cleaning us both up. She changed the sheets and blankets as I looked down at my phone. I had a few messages from my mom telling me VJ wouldn't go to sleep for her. She sent me a video at midnight and he was wide-awake. The next message came from Celeste and it was a photo of her naked. I showed it to Maylan because we don't need any secrets. She didn't say anything and told me it's for me to handle. I deleted it and blocked her which I what I should've done already.

"May, you don't ever have to worry about her again. I meant what I said about never stepping out again. You are my wife and I take my vows serious regardless of my previous history." She left out with the sheets to put in the washer but it was taking her forever to come upstairs. I threw some shorts on and went to check on her.

"What's wrong May?" She was on the couch crying.

"All of this could've been avoided if I had just told you about the pregnancy. Dante was right; I should've been a woman and talked to you about it. Instead I let your ex slither her way in your life and more than once. What the hell is wrong with me?"

"Maylan, you can't keep dwelling on the past or you're going to stress my daughter out." She looked at me.

"Your daughter. I can't be pregnant already."

"Trust me babe. I came in you a lot and put my daughter in you." She started laughing and laid her head on my shoulder. Neither of us said anything and fell asleep right there. I woke up and grabbed us a blanket and laid back on the couch. Now that May was back in my life permanently, there was no way I was letting her go.

****

Maylan and I woke up around noon the next day and she wanted to go see Isa and the kids. We picked my son up on the way and he did not want May to put him in the car seat. She had to sit in the back the entire ride to keep him calm. There's no doubt in my mind that he missed her. Shit, I damn sure did and it was way before she started messing with that fuck nigga.

I pulled up and opened the door for her to get out and stood her in front of me. My son fell asleep on the way. She wrapped her arms around my neck and stared at me. I saw the love in her eyes she used to have for me and a nigga was happy as hell it was still there. I leaned in to kiss her and she didn't stop me. We would've kept going had my son not woken up. I guess he realized the car stopped and his mom wasn't next to him.

"Baby can you carry him in? I know Katarina is going to jump on me." I told her yes and closed the door. Isa was standing there with Ariel and like she said Katarina ran out and jumped in her arms. She sat down on the step to catch her breath. Due to the stab wounds in her chest she was still a little weak.

"Where you been? I missed you. I have a big brother now and a new sister. Abel walks too and."

"God knows I missed you guys." She hugged Katarina again.

"May, it's too tight. Let go." She laughed and put her down to walk in. Abel came over and hugged her before going back to Birch. That lil boy loved him and you couldn't tell anyone that wasn't his father. I guess not, when he's all he know.

We stayed over all day and the girls cooked up a big dinner. Isa invited Dante and his family over. I know it had to do more with making Maylan come face to face with him. When they showed up Dawn gave her a hug and handed their son over. Maylan loved kids and that's why I'm about to give her a whole bunch of them.

"Dante I just want to say I'm sorry for what happened that day in the mall. Had I listened to your warning about the guy; none of this would've happened."

"It's fine but a word of advice." She looked at him.

"Don't ever let anger stand in the way of happiness. Lucky for you my boy waited for you because anyone else would've left." She gave him a hug and sat on my lap.

106

"I'm happy you waited for me."

"I told you we were never breaking up." She tossed her head back laughing. She can laugh all she wants but I meant it.

Birch

Isa woke me up around six thirty to get ready. Today she had to go down to the courthouse for an arraignment on the shit with the raid. I know she didn't sleep well and I tried to stay awake with her but I was tired. Hell, I didn't fall asleep until damn near two this morning. I know she was nervous but I paid good money for her lawyer and the detective told me they don't have much to use against her. Yes it was her place but because they had photos of guys coming in and out her apartment they knew it wasn't her shit. Plus, my moms' boyfriend is the DA and he's not about to let Isa go to jail.

I stared at her when I walked out the bathroom and she looked hella good in her blue pencil skirt, white blouse and a blue blazer over it. She had on some red bottoms my mom got her as a push gift and a Louis Vuitton purse with a Cartier watch. My mom went out her way to make sure Isa was fly going to court. Her hair had curls in it and she wore a little red lipstick that had me wanting it on my dick. She lost the baby weight and was back down to her regular size, which I think was only 170. Because she was so short people considered her fat but to me she was perfect.

"Damn baby. Let me get a quickie." I stood behind caressing her breasts through the shirt.

"As much as I need it and know for a fact it will relax me I have to focus." I backed up laughing.

"Focus on what babe? You're not going to jail and if they say you are then you know what's up." I put my Rolex on along with my shoes. I wasn't dressed up but I didn't have on jeans or boots either.

"I hope not. I don't know what I would do." She shook her hands and stared in the mirror.

"You think these expensive shoes, purse and watch will make them think I'm a drug dealer? Maybe I should go looking homeless." I fell over laughing.

"Stop laughing Birch." She had her hands on her hips.

"Isa stop worrying. I'm not going to let anything happen to you. Bring your sexy ass on before we're late." She followed me and stopped at the closet.

"You better not take those shoes or watch off." I yelled up the steps and heard her suck her teeth.

"Your man has money the legal way. Relax. I can afford

108

everything you have on so they won't question it. And before you say it, no I'm not throwing it in your face. I'm letting you know, just because you dress nice going to court, it doesn't mean you're into illegal shit." I picked up my keys and asked if she had everything and we headed out the door.

The kids were downstairs watching television with the nanny we hired. She was an older woman whose kids were married and lived out of town. None of them had kids and she came highly recommended. Isa was very nervous about her being there so we had a few nanny cams around the house. In the new place there would be cameras everywhere and could be accessed from the phone. The house would be ready in another month and she was already looking online for furniture.

"Baby."

"Relax Isa." I cut her off and turned the car off in the parking lot. I moved in closer and kissed her.

"Let's go before I have you on my lap and then we're on the news as fugitives for having sex in the parking lot." We got a kick out of the couple that had sex in a Georgia courthouse bathroom. The girl took a picture and now they're wanted like they committed a murder.

"Hey sis. You ok?" Maylan asked and gave her a hug. I noticed she wouldn't let go of Vernon's hand. I guess dude had her petrified but I can't blame her after the shit she went through.

We all walked through the metal detectors and it beeped when Isa passed. It was funny because she started panicking and trying to remove everything. The cop even started laughing at how nervous she was. Her watch was the reason it went off and as soon as she knew she looked at me, I shrugged my shoulders and took her hand in mine. Dawn, Dante and everyone we were cool with was there. On the other side of the courtroom was her pathetic ass baby daddy who I hoped to catch when we left. He and I had some unfinished business to take care of.

"Why is he here Brayden? Oh my God, is he going to say they're my drugs?"

"Isa, I may not care for him but snitching isn't in his blood. He's probably here to see what's going to happen."

The lawyer came over and had us go in a room. He pretty much repeated everything he mentioned a few days ago about them not having evidence to charge her. We went back inside the courtroom and she took a seat at the table with the lawyer. The bailiff had us all rise for the judge and I'll be damned if it wasn't my moms, boyfriends brother. I glanced over at my mom and she had a smile on her face. Isa didn't know and appeared to be nervous as the judge scanned the papers in front of him.

"Isa Harrison please stand up." The judge ordered.

"How do you plead?"

"Not guilty?"

"These are some very serious charges against you. Can you tell me how you got yourself in a situation like this?"

"I don't know how those items got in my apartment. The only thing I could assume is the person who built the place hid them there, in hopes to come back later and retrieve them. I can assure you my kids mean everything to me and I wouldn't dare have that around." He took his glasses off and stared at her before speaking to the prosecutor.

"I've gone over the evidence presented but it doesn't show Ms. Harrison doing anything wrong. I see photos here of her and a guy who could be her spouse. The other photos showing guys outside her apartment, don't seem to be doing anything either."

"But your honor. The guys in the photos are known drug dealers and the one she's in the photo with is the leader."

"Ms. Harrison, how are you affiliated with the guy in question of this photo?"

"I have two kids by him your honor." The prosecutors face turned red as if he was surprised.

"Please tell me you didn't bring this woman here because she's in photos with her kids father."

"We seized a ton of drugs, weapons and other paraphernalia in the apartment." The prosecutor was trying hard as hell to plead his case.

"I understand that and if you had some concrete evidence of her distributing something or even bringing the drugs in her home; this would have been an open and shut case. However, we're sitting here with pictures and nothing else. The woman wasn't in the apartment a year and the product and weapons could have been there previous to her moving in."

"Your honor they were brand new apartments."

"Exactly why this is a problem. The woman in question has never been arrested or in trouble, but you're telling me she's capable of handling this amount of drugs? If she is responsible for them, where are the photos of her bringing the stuff in? Do you have any photos of her distributing anything? You have to give me something." The prosecutor didn't say a word.

"Your honor, I would like all the charges dismissed against Ms. Harrison as soon as possible." Isa's lawyer said with a smile on his face.

"Motion granted. I'm sorry Mr. Prosecutor." The judge didn't even respect him enough to say his name.

"For future reference; don't come in my courtroom again with photos or drugs and no concrete evidence on who they may belong to. Yes, in the court of law the person residing there would be responsible but in this case, she was a new tenant with no criminal history and she doesn't fit the profile. Whoever you're really looking for to fall, may be in this courtroom today but until the evidence is in my face, this case is closed." He looked at Isa.

"Ms. Harrison I advise you to check your surroundings the next time you move into a place; regardless of how new it is. You were very lucky and had you been in this photo even slapping hands with the guy, you would have gone away for distribution and for a long time. Count your blessings Ms. Harrison because God was on your side today and may not be tomorrow." He banged his gavel, stood and exited the courtroom. Isa came running from behind the desk and straight to me.

"Oh my God baby. I'm not going to jail. Thank you for the lawyer and giving me the confidence to be myself. I love you and I have a surprise for you later." She kissed me and whispered some nasty shit in my ear that made me, stand her in front of me for a few minutes. Everyone congratulated her and I could tell she was relieved and I was too because she drove me crazy. My mom told us to all meet at her house for dinner and while that's all good, I'm taking my woman home to let her live out that fantasy she promised in my ear first.
　　　　　　　　**********

The next few days were perfect but with every perfect day comes bullshit and that's what I was dealing with right now sitting at this diner with Lira getting on my nerves. I didn't tell Isa about this because she would worry what temptation Lira tried which is exactly what she's doing. This woman was sucking on her finger like it was my dick. I sucked my teeth, stood up and went to the bathroom. I can admit it turned me on a little but not enough to cheat. I worked too hard to keep Isa in my life and I'm not about to allow Lira to mess it up.

I came out the bathroom and she had a big grin on her face. I snatched her ass up and went back to our seat. She kept looking down on her phone grinning.

"Lira, don't call me again until the baby is born."

"Aren't you going to offer me money to take care of myself until then?" I laughed at her.

"Not at all." I stepped out the place and noticed my phone was going off non-stop. I backed out the lot and saw Lira getting in her car.

"Yo where you at?" Vernon barked in the phone.

"Just finished talking to Lira at the diner."

"Are you trying to lose Isa?" He asked and I had to look at my phone.

"What?"

"Man, tell me you didn't fuck Lira in the bathroom."

"WHATTTTTT?" I yelled out and my phone beeped. I didn't look to see who was calling because I needed him to tell me what he was talking about.

"Lira posted a photo of you walking to the bathroom and another one with her standing outside the door. The caption under it says, *When bae wants to get freaky in the restroom. Damn I love his*" and she put a picture of an eggplant next to it."

"What the fuck? Thank goodness Isa don't have Instagram."

"She screenshot it and sent it to her. Maylan is on the phone with Isa now and bro it's not looking good for you." I ran my hand over my head as I sat in front of my moms' house. I should go home and face the music but she needs time to cool off. I finished talking to him and saw missed calls from Smitty, Dante and my mom. I looked at the text message from Smitty's phone and it was Maria cursing me out. Dawn did the same thing from Dante's phone. I don't know how I'm going to get out of this.

Isa

I can't believe he went out with Lira and didn't mention it to me. Not only that, but how did she get my phone number, is the real question? I looked over the photo she sent me a thousand times and each time tears rolled down my eyes. How could he do me like that after everything we've been through to stay together? Now his punk ass scared to come home and shacked up at his moms' house. She told me he came there explaining how the photo wasn't what it seemed but she ripped him a new asshole too. I didn't even bother to call or text because he expected it. I blocked him on the phone so even if he tried to contact me, he couldn't.

Katarina came in the room bright and early asking where he was. I sent a message to Maylan and asked if she could have Vernon pick the kids up and drop them off to Birch. I'm not trying to see him right now. Once she told me yes, I got them ready and sent the nanny home. She's not a live in one and is only there during the day unless we need her to stay longer.

My phone went off and it was a text from Abel requesting my presence. I knew it was coming once I beat the case. He smiled when I got off, which let me know he didn't want me in jail either. He gave me a time and place to meet him at some park, which is public and why shouldn't I go? Birch is meeting up with his ex so it's obvious he doesn't respect what we got, why should I?

Vernon picked the kids up not too long ago so I jumped in the shower and threw on some black jeans with a white shirt and some white Nike sneakers Birch always said looked cute on my feet. I combed my hair down, grabbed my keys and bounced. I turned the car off and walked to the bench I saw Abel sitting and was shocked to see Lique with him. He stood up and gave me a big hug. Lique was looking down on her phone as if she didn't want to speak. I don't understand women sometimes and she should've spoken first being I'm the woman helping to raise her son.

"You look good Isa." He licked his lips and she of course, sucked her teeth.

"Cut the shit Lique. At the end of the day this is the woman who has my kids and not to mention yours. For their sake it's time to focus on them." Just as he spoke my phone rang and it was an unknown number. I excused myself to answer it

"Hello."

"Where are you?" Birch barked through the phone.

"Why? Shouldn't you be more concerned with Lira?"

"Isa don't play with me. Where the fuck are you?" I had to look at my phone. He's never spoken to me that way except when he told me about the cops watching the apartment.

"My whereabouts are not your concern. The kids wanted to see you and right now I don't. Enjoy the day with them." I hung the phone up and walked back to where they were.

"What's up Abel? I know you didn't call me here for nothing." He smiled. Abel is still sexy as hell to me but I would never lie down with him again, even if I weren't with Birch.

"First off, I wanted to say I'm proud of the way you handled yourself in the courtroom."

"Why were you there?"

"Isa, I never would've allowed you to go to jail and before you ask that's all you need to know." I can't lie and say I wasn't curious but it's over now so why badger him with questions.

"Anyway, I'm here because as of lately you've been assisting in taking care of Lique's son and she's trying to do right by him but Birch is giving her a hard time. I know it's a lot to ask but can you two come up with an arrangement of some sort to make it happen?" I looked over at her.

"Is that what you want Lique?"

"He asked didn't he?"

"Hold the fuck up Lique. What the fuck you getting smart for? She's asking you and you're on some petty shit right now over the fact she's marrying your ex. If you want that nigga then you can get your shit from my house and bounce."

"Abel you know I don't want him. I'm sorry Isa, it's just that I see how much my son loves you and I want the same thing. I should've been a better mother to him but instead; going out was the only thing I worried about. We don't have to be friends but I do want a better relationship with Brayden." I heard everything she said but was still stuck on the love I saw in her eyes for Abel.

"Are you two together? And what about the baby?" I pointed to her stomach.

"Yes we are and this is Abel's daughter." I covered my mouth. I was happy in one sense but pissed in another. Here we thought Birch was having a kid by her but he's not. Thank goodness. One down and another to go. My notifications went off and it was a text from Maylan telling me Birch was looking for me. I sent a text back saying *ok* and put it back in my purse.

"When were you going to tell him?"

"Today after we finished speaking to you." I nodded my head.

"Look. Brayden loves you but he's having a hard time dealing with you and his dad not being together. Yes, he likes me but when he sees his father with my kids he thinks it's a matter of time before he's the outsider. I only know this because I sat him down and asked. He is your son Lique and I would never try and take the mother role away from you. However, you have a lot of making up to do and he's going to want you to show him more than anything." She sat there teary eyed and laid her head on Abel's shoulder. I heard my phone going off again and it was the same number Birch called me from. I hit ignore and got up to leave.

"I'll give you two a minute. I have to use the bathroom." He stood up and came close to me.

"Isa, I can never apologize enough for the way I treated you. I should've be a man about my shit and loved you the right way. I'll always love you no matter who I'm with and I promise to never disrespect you or your relationship again. I'm also sorry for bringing drugs and other shit in your house too. I was selfish and didn't think I would ever get caught. I know Abel and Katarina love that nigga but those are my kids and I want to work something out as far as seeing them." He wiped my eyes. It's been a longtime coming for him to apologize. Yea he said it before but I think it was more or less for sex. This time I felt like he meant it.

"They know who you are Abel. Birch explains the difference to Katarina when she asks. I wouldn't do that to you or them. I know how you are about your kids but you too are going to have to work for their love. It won't be as hard as it will be for her because they're still young."

"Yea I'm working on her." He smiled and shook his head.

"So you really like her huh?"

"Nah I love her. I'm not in love, but she is definitely someone I can see myself with." I turned around and she was coming out the bathroom.

"Well let me go. Take care Abel and I'll be in touch about the kids." He moved in close and kissed my cheek and things went from bad too worse just that quick. I heard a noise and it was a gun on the back of his head and Birch was holding it. I could hear Lique screaming as she came over. Abel put his hands up.

"What you on some revenge type shit Isa? I have dinner with Lira and you meet up with him? You want this nigga Isa?" He asked and hit Abel over the head with his gun and kept hitting him.

"Isa stop him." Lique screamed out as Birch dropped the gun and started beating the crap out of Abel. Vernon stood off on the side watching. After I noticed Abel looked dead, I moved closer.

"That's enough Birch."

"I told you what was going to happen when I saw him."

"Ok but I think he gets it." He pushed me back a little and I fell into one of the benches.

"You know what. I'm done with you Birch. This is the second time you put your hands on me. Stay the fuck away from me." I stormed off and I could hear him calling my name. I know it wasn't done on purpose and I probably should've moved back but Abel was on the ground. Once he heard my voice you would think he'd stop but no.

I saw Lique leaning over Abel and Vernon was holding Birch back. The entire scene was crazy but I had enough. I pulled out and went to see Maylan who must've known because she hugged me as soon as I walked in.

"No one knows you're here but you know Vernon's going to tell him." I nodded my head and told her I wanted to lie down. She came in the guest room with VJ and me and laid down. We all ended up falling asleep. I heard Vernon waking her up and opened my eyes to see Birch standing there. I rolled over on my side.

"What were you doing with him?" I scoffed up a laugh.

"Damn sure not what you were doing with your ex." I put my feet in my sneakers and grabbed my things to leave.

"I didn't do anything with her but I understand why you feel the way you did after seeing the photo. I should've told you she asked to see me, to talk about the baby. I was dead wrong Isa and I'm sorry." I stood there staring at him.

"Abel called me there to ask if I could get you to change your mind about letting Brayden spend more time with his mom. And he wants to see his kids." I watched him clench his fists.

"Why is he asking about Brayden for her and those are my kids." I didn't say anything about Abel and Katarina because he is all they know.

"They're a couple Birch and to be honest they love each other. I think it's a good idea for Brayden to spend more time with her."

"Oh now you know what's right for my son? Huh? He comes around and all of a sudden they're his kids and he should see them. Fuck out of here." He slammed his fist on the dresser.

"I'm leaving Birch. I've never seen you this angry and now you're throwing Brayden being your son in my face."

"Isa-"

"I'm the one helping you raise him. You didn't ask me one time how I felt about taking care of another woman's child but I did it because I loved you. I love Brayden too but she is his mother and if he doesn't have a problem with it, then you shouldn't either. But I see what's going on and I'm over it."

"What?"

"I'm not going to stand around and let you talk to me like shit because you're either not over your ex or you don't want to see her with anyone else. The chance of another man being in his life bothers you, but you're doing it with Abel and Katarina. You haven't once heard me speak to you disrespectfully when it came to you voicing your opinion about Abel being in their life." I stared at him and he didn't say a word.

"If you want her back, then go get her." I slid the ring off my finger, opened the door and walked out.

"Isa what's wrong?" Maylan yelled as I came running down the steps crying.

"He wants his ex back. I gave him his ring and I don't have anything else to say. I love you sis. I'll see you later." I hugged her and ran out the door.

"ISA! ISA!" I heard him yell and kept going. I don't need the bullshit. Every time something is going right in my life, another bad thing happens and I'm over it. As long as I have my kids, I'm good.

Smitty

"Man he beat the shit out of Abel and when Isa tried to stop him he pushed the shit out of her and she fell. You know what happened after that." Vernon told me after Birch went to the bathroom. I called over there once Maria hung up with Maylan and told me what went down. I know for a fact Birch loves Isa but he needs to move past this Lique phase. It has nothing to do with him wanting her. He's just stuck on the fact Abel knew she was his sons mother. But he's with Isa and regardless of him finding out late; it's the same thing. I keep telling him, Abel may have been cool growing up but he's not close to us and doesn't owe him anything.

I watched him come from the bathroom looking down on his phone with stress lines on his forehead. He's most likely trying to get in touch with Isa because he called her from all of our phones. Once she answered and he spoke; she hung up on him. He tried to get his mom to speak to her but she cursed him out too. It was a no win situation right now with him.

"I don't want Lique and now all of a sudden she wants to spend more time with Brayden and Abel wants to see the kids." He tilted the bottle up. Now I see what the problem is.

"You're mad because you thought Isa wanted him and he's going to take the kids." I asked.

"That's what I said. Wait!"

"It's cool Birch. You're in a similar situation that Vernon was in. You messed around and fell in love and you don't want her around anyone. You're attached to the kids and think the bond will be broken."

"Who are you, Dr. Phil?"

"Nah, but we all know how you feel about her and the kids. You have to talk to her about it."

"She should know."

"How? Isa can't read your mind."

"I'm ready Birch." We turned around and it was a stripper who only had on a G-string. Her breasts were perfect and she was gorgeous. Vernon and I both looked at him and shook our heads. We can say something but he's grown. He followed the chick and left us sitting there. Maria walked in with Maylan and I looked behind them to see if Isa was coming. Luckily they told me no. Maylan stood in front

118

of Vernon and Maria sat next to me.

"Where's Birch?" I shrugged my shoulders and Vernon ignored them too.

We all sat at the bar laughing and joking when I saw that nigga Martin walk in with Edie. I told Maria not to move and gave Vernon a head nod, when Kenta strolled in behind with Celeste. They couldn't see us because there was an island full of liquor bottles in the middle of the bar and the lights were dim.

"May, go with Maria to the house and I'll be there to get you."

"I don't want to leave you." She looked nervous.

"I'll meet you there babe. Maria get my wife home safe." They never got the chance to leave because shots rang out. We both dropped to the ground on top of the girls. The shooting stopped and it seemed quiet but when we looked up, we were staring down the barrel of a gun.

"Get your punk ass up." Kenta yelled out. I stood up and told Maria and Maylan to stay down.

All of a sudden a shot was fired and Kenta hit the ground. Celeste stood behind him grinning but pointed the gun down at Maylan. Vernon lost it and charged at her knocking the gun out her hand.

I punched Martin in the face and he stumbled back. Maria told me to move and shot Martin in the chest a few times. Don't ask me where she learned how to shoot but I'm not complaining. I ran over to Vernon, who had literally beaten the shit out of Celeste and grabbed him off her. He took the gun out her hand, shot Kenta a few more times, wiped his prints off and put the gun back in her hand.

"Baby get the tape." Maylan yelled out and Vernon ran to the back where the office was, kicked the door open and got it. The owner wasn't there but we've been in there plenty of times and knew where it was. This isn't our first rodeo. Everyone there knew who we were and neither of us worried about anyone snitching. I told him to take the girls out the back and I searched in every room to get Birch and he wasn't in any of them.

"Yo where you at?" I shouted in the phone when he picked up.

"I left to handle some business. What's up?" I told him what happened and he started flipping out. I told him to meet at my house and we'll discuss the rest there.

The entire ride to my house Maria asked me over and over

119

where did Edie go. It didn't even dawn on me that she disappeared. We pulled up in front of our house and Edie was standing outside her car smirking. I stepped out first and Maria came to stand on the side of me.

"What the fuck you want Edie?" I asked now that I had her yoked up by the shirt.

"I just came by to tell you, I'm leaving the state and never coming back."

"He doesn't give a fuck bitch. You should've just left." Maria was putting her hair up in a ponytail. I knew she was ready to fight but I wasn't going to let it go down like that.

"Goodbye." I said and took Maria's hand in mine.

"Don't you want to know why I'm leaving?"

"Not really."

"Well, its because I found someone else who's going to love me better and-" I slammed the door as she spoke. A few minutes later I heard glass breaking and Maria tried to run out there but I stopped her.

"Let her get it all out baby. You wanted a new car for your birthday next week right?" She stood there in the window fuming.

"Look at it this way. She did you a favor and now you'll get an early birthday gift."

"Why didn't you let me beat her ass?"

"For what Maria?" Edie threw the bat in her trunk and pulled off after her rant. I'm happy that's all she did because I really didn't want to have to kill her but I would.

"For the few years she made me miss with you." I hugged her from behind.

"Its ok. I've been making up a lot since you returned. How about we make up again?" I lifted her up bridal style and carried her up the steps. I made love to my woman as much as she let me and the time missed was a thing of the past.

Birch

"You sure this is what you want?" The stripper asked before opening the car door. I know everyone assumed I was going to sleep with this chick and had I not loved Isa, I would have. But no, this situation was different.

"I wouldn't have asked you."

"You don't have to get nasty Birch."

"Just go so I can get back to the bar before they notice I'm gone." I hadn't told anyone I was leaving and I needed her to hurry up.

"He knows I'm coming right?"

"Yea. Make sure you stick to the plan."

I watched her walk to the door and had to divert my eyes for a few seconds. Her ass was phat and the pussy good but I had to stay focused. She banged on the door and it took a few minutes for her to answer but when she did all she had on was a robe. Her and the stripper began arguing and dude came to the door, which was my cue to get out. I walked up and her eyes grew wide.

"What are you doing here Birch?"

"The question isn't what am I doing here, the question is are you fucking this nigga and supposed to have my baby in your stomach?" Lira didn't know what to say and the dude and stripper looked at her crazy.

I had someone watching Lira ever since she pulled that shit at the restaurant and sent Isa the photo. Evidently she was spending time with this guy who I know from around the way. I hit him up and asked what it was about and he told me they'd been shacking up for the last few weeks.

"Baby! Lira you never told me you were pregnant." I didn't mention it to him either because I wanted him to continue messing with her.

"Ughhhh, Birch I was going to call you and tell you I lost it."

"Lost it. Bitch you had me meet you for lunch and never mentioned it. Then you sent my girl that message making it seem like we were fucking in the bathroom. I should beat your ass."

"Yo Lira. You serious right now." The dude asked and she ran upstairs leaving us all there shaking our heads. I slapped hands with him, handed over the money, told the stripper lets go and bounced. I wasn't worried about how he felt about Lira. If he gave a shit about her he wouldn't have let it go down this way.

I doubt if the bitch was really pregnant. I did some research and the ultrasound photo didn't have a name on it and the internet said people get those pictures offline and use them all the time. The discharge papers from the hospital definitely said she was pregnant but again, I bet she used someone else's piss. I swear bitches are scandalous.

"Damn you got these bitches out here bugging. But I know why." She smirked and her hand found its way in my lap.

"Look. I appreciate you handling that for me but my girl means a lot to me and I can't get caught up."

"Lucky her and you're welcome." I dropped her off at home and my phone rang. It was Smitty telling me what happened at the club and I was pissed. At least those two niggas were no longer a threat. I told him I would be by his house later but instead went home.

I showered and laid in my bed thinking of Isa and how I keep messing up when it comes to my ex. I can say over and over, I don't want Lique but for some reason couldn't stop getting caught up in her mess. Then to find out she's with him made me angrier because she's supposed to be pregnant by me too. I wanted answers and the only way to get them was to ask.

It was midnight but I still drove to her place to find out. She opened the door and anyone could tell she was on her way out. I walked in the living room and sat on the couch.

"Is that my baby?" I cut through the chase. Her crying gave me my answer but I wanted her to say it.

"Is it?" She shook her head no.

"Why take me through all the bullshit then?"

"At first it was because I still wanted you. Once I realized you were never coming back, I left it alone. Didn't you notice I never bother you?" I listened and she was right. Lira bothered me more than her. When Lique was pregnant with my son, she called me all the time and even had me lay up with her a lot. I guess with everything going on I never paid attention.

"Whose is it?"

"Abel's." I put my head down smirking.

"Yo. This nigga is fucking connected to Isa, Dawn and now you. What the fuck?" I wasn't mad it was his baby because she can have a baby by whomever she wants. But it seems like he'll be around forever.

"You found someone who will do anything for you and love you the way you want and I did the same. I know he's the person you almost killed but he makes me happy and not ashamed to claim me." I saw her staring at me. Did she say I'm ashamed of her? Did I treat her the same way Abel treated Isa? Nah. Everyone knew about her but no one had any idea about Isa with him.

"I was never ashamed of you Lique. I wanted you to grow up and see past my money and sex. You had no goals and my son came last. If you wanted to be the wife you would have done what was necessary but everything became a game and you lost me." I took my phone out and saw Vernon text me to say we had to link up tomorrow and figure out this shit with Jared. He was still nervous about him roaming around and Maylan is scared to leave the house without him.

"You got my ex fiancé thinking I want you."

"Ex?" She seemed shocked.

"Yea man. Isa left me and I can't say I blame her. I've been so busy trying to keep you and Lira from bothering her, that I never took the time out to love her. What I mean by that is make her feel comfortable in her spot. She definitely has my heart but all this drama had me losing focus on what really matters and that's her." I put my head on the couch and closed my eyes.

"Birch can I ask you something?" Lique came in the room holding her purse and keys.

"What?"

"I want to work on having a better relationship with Brayden. I know he's getting older but it's never too late." I stared to see if she was serious.

"Lique, I swear you better want this for you and not some nigga who most likely won't be with you if you don't." Abel may be a lot of things but he was never a dead beat when it came to the kids he has with Kacey and Dawn. His issue with Isa not wanting him caused a lot of missed time with her kids.

"It was at first but then I realized, if I don't do this he'll never forgive me. I can't have my son hating me."

"Fine. We can try it out. If he-" She gave me a hug, shocking me. I moved her away because it wasn't appropriate for either of us to be that close. Not that we're attracted to the other but I myself, don't need no one busting in here thinking shit.

"Is this over between you and Abel now?" She asked walking to her car.

"Why?"

"Birch, I understand why you did what you did and he does too. Unfortunately, like you said we're all going to be connected. I'm not saying you have to be around each other but I don't want you two fighting either. There are kids involved now. Can it go back to y'all handling business separately and staying out of each other's way?"

"I'll think about it. Where you going this late anyway?" I closed the car door and she put her window down.

"To the hospital. I came home to change."

"Oh. All right then."

"Birch." I turned around.

"Yea."

"I will always love you and thanks for letting me get another chance to raise our son right. I already apologized to Isa for how I treated her but can you mention it to her again. I'm not trying to fight with her, when I know you and Abel will get on me. I may as well be cordial." I chuckled. I don't know about Abel saying something to her but I damn sure wasn't letting her bother Isa.

"I'll tell her."

"Oh. You and Vernon need to put them two in self defense classes or something."

"We don't want our women fighting Lique. You know that."

"I know but they still need to learn how to protect themselves." I waved her off and got in my car. I'll see if Vernon wants to do that. I guess it's a good idea for when I'm not around. I told her I would teach her how to fight; I guess its time.

****

It's been a week and I have yet to see or speak to Isa. I could've gone to the job but she needed space and it gave me time to get her house together. It was built and designed the way she wanted. There was nothing Isa couldn't get from me and a house was no exception.

At first she refused to let me buy her one but I lied and told her they were already building it. She believed me and instead of her speaking to an architect, I told him everything she explained she wanted in a dream house.

I went by there yesterday to open the door for the guy to do the CO. I can't even front; the house is dope. My mom wanted to see it but I told her no one could see it before Isa. It was her birthday gift and she deserves to be the first one. Of course I had to let the guy in for the inspection but that didn't count.

Today, I made plans to go get her from my moms and bring her spoiled ass home. She may not be into materialistic things but her ass is still spoiled when it comes to me. I'll give that woman my last penny if she needed it, just because. People may say it's crazy but when you love someone as much as I love her; they'll understand. I grabbed my keys and opened the door to leave.

"What are you doing here?" I asked Isa who stood in front of me with tears in her eyes. I swear she is a crybaby.

"I came by to grab some things for me and the kids." She stepped in and I grabbed her hand. I took her in the living room and sat her on my lap.

"Why are you crying? Is someone bothering you? Are you hurt?" I searched her face for an expression but only saw tears.

"What's wrong?"

"Nothing Birch. I miss you and I haven't been sleeping well. You put your hands on me and you shouldn't have. I just want you make love to me but you don't deserve it and-" I cut her off.

"I'm sorry for hurting you again. It's never intentional and I hope you know that." I wiped her eyes.

"Birch, I know when you get angry to stay away from you. I also know you had to handle the situation with Abel and had he not looked dead, I would have never stopped you. The park had a lot of people out there and I couldn't risk you going to jail. However, it doesn't excuse you putting your hands on me. I didn't deserve that."

"I know and I'm fucked up over doing it. I don't realize how hard I do it because usually one of my boys are the one who stop me. Can you come home? I miss you and my kids."

"Nope. You have to work for me to come home and to start I want the keys to the new house. I haven't been able to look inside." I laughed.

"Well, I saw it and its dope as hell. You should see the-" She put her lips on mine to stop me from speaking. I let my tongue slide in and she didn't stop me, which gave me the green light.

I stood up and went to lock the door. By the time I returned to the living room my woman was butt ass naked with a smirk on her face. I stripped out my clothes and joined her on the floor where she begged for me to fuck her. I wanted to go extra slow to enjoy the moment but its not what she wanted.

"Let me find out you are only here to get your fix." I said as she moaned in my ear.

"You're the only one who can give it to me right."

"You mean like this?" I pulled out half way and plunged back in. Her back arched, as she dug her nails in my arms and came hard.

"When were you going to tell me you were pregnant again?" I stared down at her smiling. I couldn't help but do the same. We already had four kids between us and now she's expecting again. Shit, we catching up to her ex.

"After we moved in our new house."

"I love you Isa Glover."

"We aren't married yet baby, but I love the way it sounds."
The two of us explored one another for the rest of the night. I can't lie, Isa is everything I wanted in a woman and I would die for her if it came down to it. I watched her sleep and not too long after, I did the same.

Dante

I've been searching high and low for Kacey and still keep coming up short. I told Dawn not to worry because I'm going to get her but she's not too optimistic since Kacey has been calling and taunting her like a damn kid. None of us know how she got her number but I had her change it. This guy I know kept trying to trace the number but came back with the phones were prepaid, therefore there's no way he could get her.

I, for the life of me can't understand why she's going hard for me. When we were together, she cheated and I left. Kacey didn't bother me at first; however, every now and then she'd hit me up to say hello. A year before I got with Dawn, Kacey would hit my line more and I responded once in a while but now that she knows I'm with Dawn, had a son and marrying her, she's losing it. I'll never understand how women think that if she didn't leave you, then the relationship isn't over until she says so.

"Dante, let's go to the courthouse and get married today." I turned around and Dawn had tears in her eyes coming towards me.

"Why? What's wrong?" I stood up and hugged her.

"I'm pregnant again and I don't want to keep having kids out of wedlock." I moved her back and looked in her eyes.

"You're pregnant. But our son isn't three months yet."

"I know it's sad right." She gave me a fake smile.

"I guess it's true when they say you get pregnant fast after a baby is born. Damn, my sperm strong as hell." She sucked her teeth and left me standing there grinning. I went in the room and she was feeding my greedy ass son.

"You don't want to get married now, do you?"

"What? Of course I do but you wanted a big wedding."

"I'm not worried about that. As long as you're the man standing next to me, nothing else matters." I turned her to face me and kissed her.

"When do you want to go?" She shrugged her shoulders.

"Ugh, how are you going to ask me and don't have a date in mind?"

"I just took a test and it popped in my head."

"Can we wait for Vernon to come home? I'll never hear the end of it if we do it without him." We both laughed. No matter how

127

ignorant he was, that's still my brother and I wouldn't dare leave him out.

"Let's go out to eat."

"Dante, the kids aren't dressed and-"

"Minor shit. They know how to get ready. You need to worry about how you're going to say love and obey when the reverend tells you."

"Obey. Whatever."

"Hey. That's in the vows. You have to do what it says." I shrugged my shoulders and went to leave and tell the kids to get ready.

"Get out." She threw a pillow at me.

"I command you to stop and you have to obey me." We both started laughing. I didn't think we'd make it with all the bullshit going on with Kacey but Dawn held it down. Yes, she was upset but never gave up on me. Hell yea, we can get married whenever she wanted.

The kids decided on having dinner at The Outback because they loved the onion blossom or whatever that shit is called. We picked up Lil Brayden and Katarina on the way. Kristopher was playing his game live and told him we were going out to dinner. Katarina wasn't allowing Brayden to leave her either. That's her big brother and she goes where he goes. It's crazy how Abel connects us all, and the kids are close. The entire dinner was us joking and laughing.

"I see you're having family time." I cringed when I heard her because the kids were here and I wanted to snap her neck. Dawn 's eyes were on me and she gave me a look not to bug out.

"Hi Kacey." Kristopher and Asha both said.

"Hey kids. You want to come with me and Carl?"

"No thanks. Where is my brother?" Asha asked.

"Oh he's with my mom. You sure you don't want to come. Asha, I'll do your hair the way you like."

"They said no, damn." I was getting more aggravated by the second. Why is this bitch trying to get the kids to go with her?"

"Not this time Kacey. Katarina is staying over. Do you know she is my sister too?" Kacey's entire demeanor changed.

"Kristopher and Asha get your ass up and lets go." Kacey yelled out and had people looking over in our direction. I'm not sure why Kacey spoke like that to the kids but it's about to be a problem. The look on Dawn's face was one I've never seen. It showed anger and hate. Yea, she gets mad at me but her facial expression was different.

"Are you crazy talking to my kids like that?" Dawn yelled out and put my son back in his car seat. She shocked the hell out of me and the kids. Once my son was locked in she stood up but I got in the middle

"Kacey you got to go."

"Lets go kids." Asha and Kristopher didn't know what to do and looked scared.

"Has she always talked to you like this?" Dawn asked the kids and when they said yes, out of nowhere Dawn hit her so hard she stumbled back and fell into a waiter.

"I'm about to fuck you up." Kacey screamed out.

"You're not about to hit my mom." Kristopher said and stood up with Brayden right behind him. Asha stood next to her mom and Katarina was in the chair standing up laughing. It sounds crazy so imagine how it looked.

"Wait, until I tell your father you were about to hit me." I snatched her up and drug her out to the car. I told her to sit there and I would be right back. I walked in the restaurant and the manger was asking Dawn if she was ok. Her hand was swollen and he had brought her some ice. I asked him to wrap the food up in to go boxes. We had only eaten the appetizers before she came in acting like a fool.

"Take the kids home. I'll be there in a few."

"Dante, you are not leaving with her."

"Trust me Dawn. This is what's best."

"Dante."

"It has to be done if we want peace." She nodded her head and rounded the kids up. I handed her my bankcard to pay for the food and went outside to find Kacey pouting with her arms folded in the car.

"Get out and let me drive." She sucked her teeth but did it. I drove over to her house and we both got out. There was no one outside which made it better for me to bounce later. I hit Smitty and Birch up on their cell and asked them to bring one car and pick me up. I also asked them to stop at the store and pick up some Tylenol pm pills. Neither of them asked questions because they knew we would discuss it later. Once I got the confirmation, I made my way upstairs.

"Why did you let her hit me?" Kacey asked taking her clothes off. I heard the water running in the bathroom.

"Kacey, you can't be trying to attack her every time you see her. Not only that, how are you speaking to the kids like that?"

"Fuck her." I shook my head and went in the bathroom. She had the shower running but I changed it and put the stopper in the tub.

"What are you doing?" She asked leaning on the door watching me.

"I remember how you used to take baths when you had stressful days. I would assume this is one of them." I took her hand and watched her step in. I removed my shirt, shoes and socks. I lifted my jeans and sat on the tub with my feet in the water as if it were a pool.

"Why don't you get in with me?"

"I can't go home smelling like I had a fresh shower. Let me see you play with that pussy." I had to think of something to keep her in here. She started and to be honest, it was sexy as hell. My notifications went off and it was Birch telling me they were downstairs. I told him the door was unlocked, to come in and wait for me to yell out.

"I guess your bitch is looking for you."

"Nah, that's Birch and Smitty."

"What they want?" She asked moaning out.

"They're waiting for me to drown your ass so we can make it look like an accident." Her eyes got big as hell but it was too late. I held that bitch down in the water for a good five minutes. I watched her try and get up, she scratched my arms but I had a long sleeve shirt on. Thank goodness because I didn't need my DNA under her nails. I made sure not to put my hands on her throat. This needed to look like an accident at its best.

"Yo. Did you bring the pills?" I heard those two fools downstairs arguing about something.

"Here." Smitty passed them to me. I went in the bathroom and poured a bunch in my hand. I put them in her mouth and pushed them down and far as I could but I was still unsure if it worked. I grabbed her toothbrush and forced those motherfuckers down there. I got at least seven or eight to stay. I let her body drop in the water and expected to see the pills come up but they didn't.

"Can y'all stop arguing and get up here. Damn, can't take you two fools no where."

"Fuck Birch. He talking about Maria has me on lockdown and."

"She do nigga. Why you acting like its not true?"

"Fuck both of y'all. What's up?" They came in the bathroom behind me and Smitty smirked with his perverted ass and Birch said, *"That's what she gets"*.

"Make sure we wipe down everything we touched."

"Nigga, we ain't no amateurs." Birch yelled. He's right though. We've done a lot of shit in our young days. We put it behind us and here we are doing the same thing. Hopefully, once Jared and Celeste are taken care of, it will be the last time. They've caused just as many problems and its time to rid them of the earth too.

I put my shirt, socks and sneakers on and cleaned the bathroom up. All of us went through the house and wiped down stuff whether we touched it or not. We couldn't take the chance of our fingerprints being anywhere. I looked through the window to make sure no one was coming and we all ran to the car. They dropped me off at home around eleven and the kids were asleep but my girl was right there waiting. I locked the door and jumped in the shower.

"Is it over?"

"Yup. Now come give me some head for getting rid of your problem. And before you say no, remember the word obey is in our vows."

"First of all... She was your problem to get rid of. Two... We aren't married yet, so obey my ass. And three... I'll suck your dick any day baby."

"Damnnnn, that shit sounded sexy as hell coming out your mouth. Come here?" She crawled on the bed and let her hand jerk me off while we kissed.

"She won't ever be a problem again."

"What about her son?"

"He has a father." She nodded her head and gave me the best blowjob ever. I am happy the shit with Kacey is over but I need to bring her back and kill her again if Dawn's going to give me head like this. She had my ass ready to put my thumb in my mouth, get in a fetal position and go to sleep. That's how good it was and I'm happy to know that no other man will ever know how good she is.

"You know I'm going to fuck the shit out of you tomorrow."

"I know baby but I also know, I sucked your soul out and you can't function so go to sleep."

"Oh shit. For real Dawn." She busted out laughing and I couldn't do shit but laugh with her because she was right.

Maylan

Vernon and I have been back on track now for some time and I have to admit, I love the way he loves me. We barely argue and if we do it's usually over holding my son. Isa and I now both work in the office at the condominiums and it's actually refreshing. No customers coming in talking shit nor do I have to step on peoples food and spit in their drinks. Yes, it's nasty but fuck it. People will learn that you don't fuck with the ones who handle your food.

Vernon said he had to tell me something when he got home. I was a little nervous because over the last two days he's been standoffish. I don't want to bother him too much since he's been searching high and low for Jared, who seemed to have dropped off the earth. We're married now and I hope he wasn't telling me this isn't what he wanted anymore.

"Stop worrying Maylan. I'm sure whatever it is, won't be that bad." Isa said in the phone.

"May." I heard him yelling.

"I gotta go Isa. I'll call you later." I heard Birch calling her name in the background.

"Ok. It's going to be fine." I hung up and walked downstairs. He was at the bottom of the steps with some red roses and the chocolate covered strawberries I loved. Instantly, my stomach went into knots. It's not a holiday or my birthday so what was this for? I removed the stuff from his hand and he led me in the other room but asked where his son was first. I told him upstairs.

"Come here May." He sat on the couch and pulled me down on his lap.

"What's Wrong Vernon? You're making me nervous." He ran his hand down my face.

"First off, I want to say, I love the hell out of you Maylan and as you know, there's nothing I wouldn't do for you."

"Ok. Now you're scaring me."

"Maylan when you went with that dude after I asked if he put his hands on you, I had to do what I had to, in order to find you."

"Okkkk. What did you have to do?"

"Celeste sucked my dick in the bathroom at the bar." He held me tight when I tried to get up. I wasn't angry with him getting head because it was to locate me but why did it always include her.

"Vernon why do you keep running to her?"

"May, I promise you it wasn't like that. Me and the guys were at the bar and she came in. She wouldn't give me your whereabouts unless I let her do something sexual with me."

"Ok, I understand, I guess." I mean what could I really say? We weren't together.

"That's not it." I heard someone knock on the door but he wouldn't let me get it.

"Vernon someone's at the door."

"Maylan, I need to tell you something." He looked stressed.

"Please don't tell me you slept with her and she's pregnant."

"Nah, but the night she sucked my dick, I promised to try and make it work with her if I found you."

"Is that her?" I jumped up and went to the door. Birch stood there with Isa and two cops.

"Vernon what's going on?" He came to me.

"Celeste called me the other day."

"I thought she was dead." I whispered but he heard me.

"She made it and said if I didn't make good on my promise, she was calling the cops and tell them who did that to her."

"Is that why they're here? Are they taking you to jail?" I pointed to the cops.

"May, I told her no and if I had to go to jail, it is what it is. I wouldn't dare hurt you again."

"But there's no proof." I felt the tears coming down my face.

"Stop crying May."

"Vernon you can't leave me. What about Jared coming to find me? What about VJ? Vernon please." I was breaking down.

"Maylan, I want you to pack you and VJ up and stay with my mom or you can stay with Isa and Birch. I don't want you here in this house alone."

"Vernon please." I made my way over to the officers.

"Excuse me officer. I'm the one who attacked Celeste. He was taking up for me. I kicked her in the face over and over." I held my arms out for them to handcuff me.

"MAYLAN ARE YOU CRAZY?" Vernon snatched me back.

"I don't want you to go to jail. I'll go. Jared can't get me in there. Take care of VJ."

"Maylan I'm going to beat this." He held my face in his hands and rested his forehead on mine.

"I love you for trying to take the charge but I would never allow my wife to sit in jail. Get your stuff to go."

"Vernon come with me. I don't want them taking you while I'm upstairs." He looked at the officers and they shrugged their shoulders. He came behind me and took a suitcase out the closet.

"Vernon let's go out the window. We can grab VJ and never look back. Please baby. I can't be here without you." I was hysterical by now. He stopped putting things in and stared at me.

"Maylan, I'm going to jail because she pressed charges and has text messages with me saying if she doesn't leave me alone, I'm going to kill her."

"I thought you blocked her after she sent that photo."

"This was right after you had my son. She kept the messages and is now using them against me. They don't have the video from the night at the bar so it isn't much they can do. Maylan I should be home in a day or two."

"But-" He pressed his lips on mine.

"I want to make love to you May." He backed up. I removed my clothes, locked the door and let him have his way with me. I'm not sure how long we were in there but Birch came knocking on the door.

"Make me cum for you. You know how." He said as I rode him. I got on my feet and did my famous move on his dick and he came instantly.

"Damn, I love you."

"I'll be right out Birch. Come take a shower with me." He grabbed my hand and we took a quick one together, got dressed and headed down stairs. He carried the suitcases while I brought my son.

"Go ahead. I don't need her seeing them put cuffs on me and get even more upset." I heard him say to Birch. He walked me to the car and kissed me and VJ. I couldn't stop crying and stared out the back window as Isa drove us away. Birch stayed back because he was meeting up with the lawyer at the jail. As soon as my life starts to get on the right track, this bullshit happens. I'm going to get Celeste if it's the last thing I do and I'm going to use the one person I never expected to see again.

****

I've been staying with Vernon's mom since he's been locked up. It's never a problem because I loved her like my own. She helped me a lot with VJ and I appreciated it. However, I missed my husband but it's time to get down to business. Vernon is going to be mad, but I have to do what I have to.

"Hey honey. I missed you." My mom said when I got to her house. I left VJ with his other grandmother so I could handle her ass.

"Don't hey honey me. Why would you treat my husband like that?" I went in the bedroom I had there and scanned it, to see if I needed anything, which I didn't.

"So you really are married to him?"

"Yes I am, and I'm proud of it. What I can't understand is why you were trying to get him thrown out the hospital room after everything he's done for me."

"Maylan, his excess baggage is what keeps putting you in there. Now if I were you-" I stopped her right there.

"That's the exact problem I have with you and anyone else who feels like judging me. Yes, in the beginning I dealt with a lot from his drama but not once did he leave me hanging or put me out. He continued taking care of me, even before finding out about my pregnancy.

Isa and I were out in that shed for over a year and you couldn't find it in your heart to do the right thing and get your shit together to make sure I was ok. Yes, I was grown but ma, you tried to sell me to the highest bidder. If I hadn't run away, Vernon and I would've never met, I wouldn't have my son or possibly my life."

"Now you're being dramatic Maylan." She plopped down on the couch smoking a cigarette.

"Ma, you had me scared to leave my own bedroom because you and daddy would be so high, I never knew if a man was waiting for me. What type of parents do that to their kids?" She didn't say anything.

"Exactly! As always you have nothing to say when I call you out on your shit. As far as me recently being in the hospital. That was a decision I made on my own. Did you even find out what happened or were you too busy trying to belittle and disrespect my husband?"

"I didn't need to find out. I'm sure his ex had everything to do with it."

"She did but not for reasons you think." She sucked her teeth.

"Vernon and I were separated ma." She turned to look at me with a shocked expression.

"I met a man who in the beginning became a distraction from Vernon. He treated me like a Queen for the first couple of weeks but then he turned into this monster. He beat on me so much that this last time; he almost killed me, which is why I was in the hospital. Ma, I have dentures in the top of my mouth, half of my bottom teeth are capped and I have scars mentally and physically from the abuse." I lifted my shirt up and she looked at the scars in horror. Granted, they looked like I had been branded by a fraternity but my man didn't mind.

"I couldn't tell anyone what was going on and by the time they figured it out, I was half dead. I refused to tell Vernon the truth and yet, he never gave up on me. You talk so much shit about him and yes, it was a mess in the beginning but he is the one who found me. So yes, he had every right to be by my side. I will go to hell and back for him and in return, he'd do the same and has proven it because he's in jail right now, with attempted murder charges on his ex."

"Hmph. Why did it take this long for him to try and kill her?"

"You don't get it do you? This man saved me from being homeless, from almost dying and when I tried to take the charge he wouldn't let me." She gave me a disgusted look.

"What is going on with you and Isa? It's like you feel you owe them for rescuing you, so you're doing anything they ask and allowing them to treat you like shit." I shook my head at her. She would find anything wrong with what I said at this point.

"Rescuing us was all we could ask for. Falling in love with Vernon is a bonus because my son and future kids came and will come from him. Maybe if you get off that pedal stool you put yourself on and come back to reality, you'll see how good of a man he is to me." I grabbed my keys and headed to the door. I turned around and she hadn't moved.

"You know, I had high hopes for you when you went to rehab. I thought we could be this big happy family and forget about the past but you're never going to change. You will always be the woman who finds faults in what everyone else does but not within you. Tell my father I love him and will be by to pick him up for dinner tomorrow."

"I can't come." I laughed.

"Nah. I can't have you talking negative about my husband around his son and honestly, until you come to grips with all the shit you did in life, you'll never move forward and I don't want to be around you."

"You're father is no better than me." She screamed out when I opened the door.

"You're right but he's not in denial about anything and we're

136

closer now then we've ever been."

"How is that? You don't come here." I had to laugh at her once again.

"No, but he's been to my house, had dinner with me and my husband and we've taken him to his meetings a few times. Something you stopped going to after you got out." She sucked her teeth.

"Are you using again?" I asked and looked in her eyes that appeared to be glossy now that I took a better look. It could be that she was about to cry.

"No, but if I were, its none of your business. I'm grown."

"Exactly, and so am I. Goodbye mother." I slammed the door and walked outside. I had an eerie feeling over me; similar to the night Celeste attacked me. I looked around and a few of the guys out there waved at me and one came running over. His name was Alex and the two of us used to hang out at the park playing basketball a lot. He is in the street life now and I'm on the other side of town so we didn't see much of each other.

"Hey stranger." He gave me a hug and backed up.

"Congratulations on the baby."

"Thanks and same to you. I heard you had two already." He laughed.

"Alex!" Some chick yelled and he rolled his eyes.

"Listen, some guy came by here asking questions about you." When he said that I knew it was Jared. He's never been to my moms' house but he was aware of where it was located. I asked him to describe the person and sure enough it sounded like him.

"Anyway, I almost shot his ass for saying disrespectful shit about you."

"Huh?"

"Yea. He came out here saying some shit about you being a ho and sleeping with some other nigga while you're pregnant with his kid. I know you ain't doing no shit like that so I gave him a warning to get the fuck out of here. He hasn't been back since but you need to watch your back."

"Alex."

"WHAT! I'll be there in a minute, damn." He yelled at the chick.

"Listen, I know your man is locked up and his boys are cool with you but if you need assistance in anything let me know." I thanked him and had him put his number in my phone.

"I may need you soon so expect my call."

137

"You got it sis." We hugged and he made his way back to the chick as I went to my car. I still had the feeling so I called Birch up and asked him to meet me at the store. The purpose is for him to follow me home to make sure no one else is following him. He is good with that shit and right now I didn't need any nonsense around my son. I wanted to get this shit over with Jared and have my man where he belongs.

Abel

"Is Abel here?" I heard his voice but I know my ears had to be playing tricks on me in order for this nigga to be at my door. I made my way in the living room and could hear the two of them going back and forth.

"Ain't nobody over here trying to fight him."

"Then what do you want?" Lique had her arms crossed in front of her and leaning on the door. It was funny as hell to see her protecting me from her ex.

"It's all good baby. We have unfinished business to handle."

"Mmmmm hmmm. I'm staying right here. I swear Birch you and Abel better control that damn testosterone. You both got who you wanted and fighting should be out of your system."

"Be quiet Lique." We both said at the same time.

"Fuck y'all." She gave us the finger and sat on the couch.

"Look. We ain't ever going to be cool like we used to be but I do know you're a street nigga with connections."

"I'm listening." I sat next to Lique and she put her head on my shoulder.

"I'm not sure if you heard but your boy Jared did some crazy shit to Maylan and now he's missing. We need to find his ass fast because he's under the assumption she's carrying his baby and we need to keep it that way to bring him out. However, he hasn't showed his face since he snuck in the hospital."

"He what?"

"Exactly and Vernon isn't happy." I couldn't believe Jared was acting crazy over a woman he tried to kill.

"Why would I help you?"

"I think this is enough to peek your interest." I reached for the envelope he gave me and it was a discovery on the raid at Isa's place. I became enraged when I saw Jared's name all over it. I knew there was a snitch because in all the years I've been in the game, we've never been caught. Why would he do me like that after putting him on? I swear motherfuckers hate to see the next man winning when it comes to making money.

"Celeste should know where he is." Lique said and we both looked at her. I felt her looking over my shoulder at the papers so I'm sure she knew I'd be willing to help at this point.

139

"We believe Celeste got Vernon locked up on purpose, to give Jared room to get Maylan."

"Oh my God. What the hell is going on? I know Vernon is mad."

"He doesn't know Lique. He thinks she pressed charges because he doesn't want to be with her but if Jared gets Maylan, after this so called baby is born, he is going to kill her. Celeste believes if she's out the picture, he'll take her back."

Lique started telling us about what happened at the restaurant one day and it never dawned on me that his ass was up to no good.

"In the beginning he portrayed their relationship as perfect. I had no idea he was doing all that to her. The day he came here and said he tried to kill her, I told his ass he better leave because Vernon would find him. I guess he didn't listen. The only person who would possibly know where he's at is Celeste."

"When's the last time you talked to her?" Birch asked Lique who said a week ago. She called to tell her Kacey was still bugging about Dante not wanting her.

"I can call and ask her to meet me and say I want her to go baby shopping with me." We both looked at her.

"No Lique. You're pregnant and-" I said.

"Birch, tell him I'll be fine."

"That's your man. I can't tell him to make you do shit. I wouldn't let Isa do it either." He leaned back and tapped away on his phone.

"Come on Abel. This will be my way of making up for all the mean shit I did to them."

"No Lique." She folded her arms and started pouting. I hated when she did that and she knew it.

"Be careful when you talk to her. If you piss her off, she's going to walk. We need her to locate him." I told her after finally giving in.

I have to admit when Birch came over; I thought we'd be throwing hands again. We've been through a lot of shit and now here we are trying to work together to get this stupid nigga. I picked the phone up and called my boy at the jail and had him give Vernon a private visit with Maylan because Birch said she was going up there and wanted to tell him. There's no way she could mention it on those phones.

After the visit he called me and I told him to put me on the phone with Vernon, who acted exactly how I knew he would. I understood though because Maylan is his wife and the thought of anything happening to her is most likely driving him crazy.

After I hung up on his hostile ass, Lique told us Celeste would meet her. Which gave us time to get everything in order. Birch got up to leave and I walked him to the door with Lique on our heels like a damn stalker. I can't lie though, I loved the way she loved me.

"Look, I know you're attached to Katarina and Abel-" I started to say but he stopped me.

"Isa already ripped me a new asshole over this so if you don't mind, I don't want to talk about it. What I will say is, I know how you are with your other kids so I'm not worried about them being with you. I don't expect you to ignore my son either. If you two are a couple, treat him as if he were yours, the same way I'm doing yours."

"Birch why would you say that? He wouldn't do any shit like that."

"She hasn't been the best mother so I'm making sure he'll be treated good by someone over here." She sucked her teeth but didn't really have the right to be mad.

"That's never been an issue. Kids don't have anything to do with their parents disagreements."

"Oh, one other thing."

"That's one thing you don't have to worry about here. This house will never have drugs in it. And tell Isa; I apologize again for putting her in that position and getting arrested. It was never my intention and I'm happy my kids weren't there."

"That's all I needed to hear. Isa said the kids would be here when this is all over because she wants me all to herself. And the wife always gets what she wants, sooooo I suggest y'all get ready because those kids are bad as hell."

We all busted out laughing.

"What about Ariel?" Birch sucked his teeth. How the hell did she even know what the baby's name was?

"My mom will have her."

"What's that about?" Lique was being nosy as hell.

"Nothing. She come around too much and don't be letting me hold her." Lique laughed.

"She used to be the same way with little Brayden." He shook his head and walked out.

"You should call Dawn and Kacey for them to bring the kids too. Brayden and Kristopher are tight now and Asha loves Katarina.

Plus, it would be nice to have all the kids. It could be one big slumber party."

"Whatever you want Lique but they ass having pizza for dinner."

"Why can't we go to the movies and eat out?"

"With all them damn kids?" She gave me the side eye.

"They're yours. And you got this one coming too."

"We'll see. Let's get this shit over with them first." She kissed my lips and we sat on the couch watching some movie on the fire stick.

****

"Fuck!!" I jumped up out the bed when I got the phone call. Lique turned over with a nervous look on her face.

"Abel what's wrong?"

"Throw some clothes on. I'll tell you in the car." She did what I asked without badgering me with questions. I heard the shower going and hopped in with her. It may be four in the morning but after the news I got, I'm sure it's going to be a long day. I kissed her stomach and stared at her.

"I really do love you Lique."

"I believe you Abel. You may not be in love with me and that's fine, but I do know you love me and your daughter." No other words were spoken as we finished and our clothes on.

"Lique, I know this relationship is new but my son will be staying with us."

"Which one?"

"You know damn well Dawn or Isa ain't having that." We both laughed.

"My son Carl." I hated Kacey for naming him after her father. He didn't have to be a junior but she could've picked a better name.

"Ok. We have to get stuff for the room and go shopping for clothes." That's exactly why I loved her. She was a down ass chick and I'm glad Birch messed up with her.

"They found Kacey dead in her house. Her sister went by after the club or some shit and found her."

"Oh my God Abel. Are you ok?" She put her hand in mine.

"I really don't know how to feel right now. Kacey was being selfish to my son doing this dumb shit but what can I do now?"

"All you can do is be there for him at this point. He's going to ask a lot of questions about her."

"How do you know?"

142

"Isa."

"Isa." She snickered.

"Yes. I've been talking to her about Brayden and the things he likes and doesn't. The way he separates his food on his plate because he doesn't like it to touch; things like that. It's not the same but when he asks questions about me she gives him the best answer she can. And you'll have to do the same."

"You don't know that?" I was confused on why she didn't know much about her own kid.

"To be honest, he was with his grandmother a lot. I would give him cereal for breakfast or we would eat take out. I missed out on a lot Abel and to see another woman caring for my son bothers me. It's nothing against her because I respect her even more for doing it. I should know those things and I don't." She started tearing up.

"Well all you can do now, is focus on the future with him and do better. I'll be right there to help you."

"Really."

"You're my woman now Lique and ain't no way in hell you'll be neglecting your mother duties." I don't know how Birch allowed it to go on but then again he took him from her so it didn't matter.

"Isa is a damn good mom and I know for a fact she's treating Brayden as if he's her own."

"She is. Brayden calls her mama Isa but she wouldn't allow him to until she spoke to me. Most women would just let it happen. I'm happy she's filling me in n everything. I'm not saying we'll be best friends because I did some foul shit to her. However, this is about Brayden and nothing else." I nodded my head and continued driving. Who knew Lique's crazy ass would grow up? I thought she would always be ghetto and loud but seeing this side of her, is refreshing. No one wants a woman who causes problems everywhere they go.

I parked outside of Kacey's house and it was a few cop cars, the coroner's truck and the damn newspaper people. Lique got out with me and I took her hand in mine as we made our way to the officers and the detective who was next to them. I explained who I was, as if they didn't know, and asked where my son was. They told me no one was in the house with her and that she drowned. He also told me she had a few pills on the side of the tub, which gave them the impression that's what she took. They couldn't say what pills they were though. The detective gave me his card and a smirk along with it.

"You got off in that raid but I'm still going to be watching you." I tossed my head back laughing.

"Be my guest, but you know I'm smarter than that. Now, that I know who the snitch was, its going to be hard." His smirk turned to a frown and he stormed in the other direction. I hate when they thought you would buckle under pressure with the bullshit. I saw Kacey's mom, along with her sister who called me, and a few of her other relatives standing by a car.

"Why the fuck do you have my son out here?" I screamed at her when I saw Carl in the backseat asleep in pajamas.

"Abel don't come over here talking shit. They came to see what happened and-" Her sister said before I cut her off.

"You mean to tell me that none of you could stay home with him?"

"Abel, how dare you come out here yelling at us when you brought your whore with you? Weren't you and my daughter friends? Did you do this so my daughter would be out the way for you to be with him?" Her mom asked Lique and then looked her up and down. I stepped directly in front of her. Lique was about to say something but I told her to let me handle it.

"First off... Don't ever come for my girl. Second... her and Kacey were acquaintances that met through her best friend Celeste, who I did indeed fuck quite a bit. So if you want to be mad at one of her friends, be mad at her." None of them said a word.

"As far as my girl being a ho, she is far from it. Now your daughter, hmph, she has a track record of fucking other peoples men and destroying homes because she can't handle being alone. Before you start blaming people for what the cops are claiming to be a suicide, think about what she had going on in her life, and why she may have done it, before you start talking shit. And you." I pointed to her sister.

"You of all people knew exactly how Kacey was."

"Be quiet Abel." She said turning her back.

"Oh, you don't want anyone to know you had a piece of this good dick too. I mean you were willing to tell Kacey about it, unless I supplied you with it."

"What?" Her mom yelled out.

"So what, you have community dick?" Her mom asked and stared at Kacey's sister.

"Yup and if a bitch wants it, I'm going to give it to her." I felt Lique squeeze my hand.

"Well not anymore, but before it didn't matter who she was. Oh, and I kept it wrapped up before you assume I have AIDS or some shit The only ones I didn't with are the ones who have my kids."

"Fuck you Abel. My sister is dead and you're talking about who you fucked."

"That's your miserable ass mama. Anyway, move so I can get my son."

"Abel, you're not taking him." I laughed and opened the door. I picked him up and laid him on my shoulder. I grabbed Lique and started to walk away.

"Abel."

"What?" I walked back to her mom.

"If you think for one minute you're keeping my son in hopes of me sending you a check, you're sadly mistaken. He is my son and will be living with me. And before you even think about coming for me, which I can tell by your eyes, you're thinking about it. Remember, who the fuck I am and make sure your life insurance is paid up."

"Is that a threat Abel because the cops are right there and-"

"And you can tell them what I said. They don't fuck with me so it really doesn't matter. Stay the fuck away from me and if I want him to see you, I'll make the call." And with that said, I walked away with my woman, my son and a peace of mind from Kacey ever bothering me again. I feel bad she took her life but it was her choice. My son will suffer in the long run but as long as his dad has his back, he'll be good.

Lique

After waking up early this morning to find out Kacey took her life, it was as if we were running around all day. We got back to the house around six and both of us got in the bed and laid Carl in the middle with us. He's been here before but Abel wanted him near in case he woke up looking for his mom and wondering why he was here, and not at his grandmothers where he fell asleep. Lucky for us, he didn't wake up until after eight, which seemed to revive us. I made breakfast, which included pancakes, eggs, bacon and grits. Yes, I know how to cook, regardless if I did it or not.

Abel gave him a bath and had a talk with him about Kacey. I wanted to cry as I stood in the doorway listening to him try and explain that he wouldn't see his mom anymore. Carl asked him over and over why, but all he could come up with is God wanted her back. He didn't seem to upset but I'm sure once he doesn't see her for a while, it will hit him. He's a kid and we tend to think what bothers us, doesn't bother them but I beg to differ.

Once we all got dressed my phone stated ringing. I looked down at it and it was Celeste. Abel told me to answer it and when I did, it was just my luck she had heard about Kacey and wanted to hang out. I declined at first but Abel reminded me that I begged him to hit her up for information and if it meant today, then it is what it is. I called her back and told her to meet me at the mall. Abel gave me some money to pick things up for Carl and the baby. I sent a text to Birch to let him know the plan was moving forward and where I would be.

"Hey bitch! Long time, no see. Now that you're boo loving it up with Abel ain't nobody heard from you." Celeste said when she came in kids' foot locker. She text me and asked what store I was in when she got here.

"Girl bye. You were obsessing over Vernon and coming up with schemes to get rid of Maylan. By the way how is that going?" I looked at her face and Vernon had done a number on her. You could tell she was still in pain by the limp she had. Her face wasn't swollen but she had a few scars on it from what looked to be where stitches could have been. There was a brace on her arm and her nose was crooked, or at least it seemed to be.

"Fuck that bitch. She's about to get what's coming to

her soon enough."

"Celeste, you need to get over the fact that Vernon is never going to be with you. Not only does he have a son with her, but she has his last name and he got her a house, a car, gave her an endless bank account and so forth."

"Too bad she can't have his dick. I had his ass locked up so Jared can get to Maylan." I covered my mouth in shock as if Birch didn't tell me that was her plan all along. She went on to tell me as we stepped out the store how Jared planned on snatching her one-day when she least expects it and keep her hostage until she delivers his baby. After she does, is when he's going to kill her. I couldn't believe the two of them were obsessing like this.

"What you doing when you leave here?" She asked and I told her nothing.

"Good. Ride with me over to Vernon's old spot. I need to pick some things up I left there."

"Are you crazy?" I yelled out and then thought in my mind that this was perfect.

"Relax Lique. I'm just getting some of Maylan's clothes to wear for court in a few days. I may not like her, but he had her rocking some fly shit. Since, she'll be dead soon, I may as well get a wear out of them."

"Girl, you are crazy." I told her but stayed with her walking around the mall for another hour. I sent Birch a text and he told me to hold her there as long as I could in order to get ready. I don't know what he had up his sleeve and I didn't care at this point. She is toxic and the faster she gets out of my life, the better. Celeste used to be my friend and I had her back but once her obsession started I found myself distancing myself from her.

She helped me put the bags in the car and I drove her to the one she came in, which wasn't hers. I asked whose it was and of course, it belonged to Jared. She pulled in Vernon's driveway with me behind her. Abel was on the phone with me the entire time telling me to maintain my distance once we stepped in the house.

I guess Birch called him and he was worried. This bitch walked up on the steps and believe it or not, her key still worked. I guess Vernon didn't care if she had the key being he had brought Maylan a brand new one and stayed there. She had this wicked grin on her face as she stepped inside.

She peeked around the house and it was quiet as a

mouse. I walked up the steps behind her and started smirking when I noticed some of Maylan's things. Celeste opened the bedroom door and went straight to the closet. She wasted no time pulling out clothes and even shoes to try and match with it. If this bitch made it to court and Vernon peeped the clothes she wore, he would go ballistic knowing she was in the house.

The look on her face when she saw the sheets on the bed were messed up was priceless. She started talking to herself about how Maylan could never love or fuck him the same and a bunch of unnecessary shit. Abel was texting me the entire time, making sure I was ok. I told this bitch to hurry up since she got out the funk she was in and started trying clothes on. This bitch was really pushing it.

"Still trying to be me, huh?" I jumped when I heard the voice. Celeste and I both turned around to see Maylan dressed in all black. She wore a ponytail but the hair was wrapped up with none dangling. She had on some black Timberland boots and her face was shiny. *Did this chick have Vaseline on her face?*

"Bitch bye. Don't nobody want to be you. All this time it's been the other way around." Celeste continued trying on a pair of shoes as if Maylan's presence didn't bother her. I stepped out the room and face timed Abel like he asked without Celeste knowing. His crazy ass wanted to see too.

"You do know this obsession over my husband isn't healthy." Maylan walked closer to her.

"Bitch, your husband will be grieving you soon so don't get too comfortable."

"And why is that?"

"Because-" Is all Celeste was able to get out before Maylan punched her in the face so hard; she fell on the edge of the bed and then on the floor.

"Oh shit Maylan." Birch came in the room yelling with Dante and Smitty too.

"Back up Lique. You are too close." I heard Abel saying but shit, the guys were blocking my view. By the time I stood on the bed to see, Maylan was on top of Celeste punching her over and over with what looked like brass knuckles. She stood up and kicked her in the stomach a few times.

Out of nowhere Maylan grabbed a metal baseball bat from Smitty's hand, which I didn't notice until she did and lost it on Celeste. I mean she hit her in the head so many times, I'm sure her skull was crushed. Her face was mangled and I saw teeth on the ground. Maylan hit her over and over as if she was in a zone. I've never seen this much blood in my life.

"That's enough May. I think she's dead." Dante lifted her away from Celeste and drug her out the room as she cried. I could hear her saying she didn't get her to sign the paper. How was Vernon going to come home?

"Now what?" Smitty said.

"Now we make it like it was a break in and it is what it is. Someone could've followed her here."

"Don't worry about it. I already have someone on their way over." Abel said shocking the hell out of us.

"Word!" Smitty said staring at the phone.

"Lets just let bygones be bygones and remain cordial to one another. Lique is my woman and she is an accessory to what happened and I'm not about to let her go down. You have as much to lose as I do. You need to get out of the house ASAP and tell Maylan not to worry about the letter. Lique can sign Celeste name on it and I will have it notarized first thing in the morning."

"Yo, how much?" Birch said not believing what was really happening.

"Don't insult me. I said the past is the past. Our kids will be around each other for the rest of their life so we may as well get over the bullshit. Now hurry up and get out of there. My men are on their way and I hope that's not a spot Vernon wanted to keep because it will be ashes when they're done." Abel told them.

"Dante, Vernon is never going to come home." I heard Maylan saying when we walked down the stairs. I felt bad seeing her so upset. She had blood on her clothes and he handed her paper towels to wipe it off her hands.

"You think Abel can get her in the jail to see him?" Dante asked and I called Abel. He said he would make some calls and try to make it happen. In the meantime, I told her whatever letter she was referring to would be signed and notarized to help Vernon get out. Shockingly, she gave me a hug and said thank you.

"And you couldn't stand her in the beginning." Smitty said with his smart ass.

"Whatever punk. Lets go. We have to be out before his people come." I said reminding them. We all took some towels out the bathroom and wiped down the things we touched and Birch took the bat and Maylan out the house. I got in my car and headed to the house with Abel. Today has been one hell of a day and I'm glad its over. Now all they had to do was get this punk Jared and it would really be all over.

Vernon

Two days before I got locked up Celeste called me from an unknown number. Once I heard her voice I hung up but she kept calling back. I finally answered and she tried her hardest to get me to incriminate myself over the phone when I told her no on being with her. I'm no fool and luckily I didn't because the next day Detective Will hit me up and asked me to stop by his store. I couldn't go to the office because the information he gave me could've gotten him fired. He pulled me in the back and gave me the run down of Celeste coming in the station filing charges. The only thing on my mind was murder and how Maylan would take me leaving her.

Leaving my wife and son had to be the worst day of my life. Yea, I took her through a lot of unnecessary bullshit, but in all relationships, you have to go through something, in order to see what you need is right in front of you. She was hysterical and it was tearing me up on the inside. However, if she saw me breaking it would've been worse.

I was supposed to be out of here in a day or two but here it is two weeks later and I'm still here. The judge denied my bail because the idiot Celeste claimed she feared for her life and some other bullshit. My wife is supposed to visit me today because she had something important to tell me, that couldn't be said over the phone. At first, I wouldn't allow her up here but after hearing the way she spoke last night, I could tell something wasn't right. I heard the CO call my name for the visit.

When I walked in the room they told me to go in a different one. I thought we would have to speak through the phone but somehow we're in a room with just my son and us. It was all cement, with no cameras or two-way mirrors. Maylan stood there looking as beautiful as ever. I could see the bags under her eyes from not sleeping and crying but it didn't matter because she's still perfect.

"I missed you so much baby." She hugged me and we engaged in a deep kiss. We stopped when VJ started whining. She and I talked about what was going on at my moms' house. Not once, did she bring anything up about why she was upset last night and the reason for her being here.

"How much longer? I want my husband home."

"Not much longer. The court date was pushed up."

"How?"

"My lawyer is cool with the new judge on the case and got it moved up. May, all they have is her statement and text messages. There's no DNA of mine on her and they have the messages from my phone with her trying to blackmail me."

"But if they have them, why can't you go home?"

"She claims to be scared."

"You won't have to worry about her soon." I heard her mumble.

"Mr. Davis time up." I told him one minute.

"Maylan what are you talking about?"

"Nothing."

"I swear to God you better not do anything crazy. I can't take it if anything happened to you and I'm in here."

"I'll be fine Vernon." She took VJ from me.

"Maylan Davis." She smiled when I called her with my last name.

"Vernon, she has done enough of hurting us and its time she pays for it." She whispered and I snatched her arm.

"Leave it alone baby, please. I'm begging you May. If anything happens."

"It won't. Please trust me. I need to know you have faith in your wife to help you, the same as you have done for me." I grabbed her hand that was on my face and kissed it.

"Take Birch or Dante with you."

"Vernon you worry too much." She smiled and walked out the door.

"MAYLAN!"

"I love you Vernon. Don't ever forget that."

"MAYLAN! MAYLAN!" I tried to run after her but the guards stopped me.

"FUCKKKKKKK." I need a damn phone. The CO pulled me in my cell and handed me a phone. I gave him a crazy look and he told me to speak.

"Who the fuck is this?"

"She'll be fine Vernon. There will be someone with her every step of the way."

"If she even has a scratch on her, I will find you and take your life in front of your kids."

"Still the same violent nigga."

152

"What the fuck you say?"

"Calm your hostile ass down. I understand you're stressed but this is something she felt she had to do. Have faith in your wife Vernon because I can tell you right now; if I stop her she's going to do it anyway. At least she'll be protected this way."

"Why did she come to you?"

"She didn't. Birch did." And with that he hung the phone up. What the hell is going on? I had to get the fuck out of here and fast.
****

A few days went by and I hadn't heard from my wife or any of my boys. My mom brought my son up and told me Maylan was ok and I had to trust her.

I trusted my wife, no doubt, but I don't trust the motherfuckers out there. If Birch went to Abel, then it must be something big and he needed his assistance because I can't see them working together after everything that went down. I think it pissed me off not knowing what was going on.

"Yooooo did you here they found one of Abel's kids mother dead." Some guy from around the way said.

"Oh word."

"Yea. They said she committed suicide. She took a bunch of pills and they found her under water in the tub." I can't confirm or deny but I bet my life it was Dante. He started telling me all the other shit going down in the hood. I had to hurry up and get the hell out of here.

I went in my cell and laid down looking up at the bottom of the mattress on the top bunk. There was a photo of May and my son she sent me that was taken before that fuck nigga got her. It bothered me that she didn't want help but more or so that I couldn't save her before it got bad. I may have rescued her but those memories will be in her mind forever. I tried to call her all night and she denied my call each time. I ended up forcing myself to sleep, otherwise I was going to take my anger out on everyone and if I planned on getting out of here; I had to stay under the radar.

I felt someone shaking me out my sleep and turned around to find the same CO standing there. It had to be late because all the lights were out in the jail and it was quiet. He put his finger to his mouth and told me not to say anything but to follow him. I told him to give me a second because I had to use the bathroom. After I finished and cleaned my hands in that little ass sink, he escorted me to some room where I

153

came face to face with my wife. How in the hell did she get in here this late is beyond me but at least I know she's ok.

"What the fuck May? Why didn't you answer your phone?"

"Vernon, I can't stay long but I had to see you. I'm sorry for not answering but I couldn't lose focus on what needed to be done. Had I spoke to you, you would've tried talking me out of it."

"What did you do May?"

"I did what I had to, for you."

"Is it going to put you behind bars?" She dropped her head and I lifted it back up with my hand.

"That's why I wanted you to wait. I can't take a charge for something you did, if I was in here when you did it. Baby, do you know how much I love you?" She nodded yes.

"Then know I would've handled it."

"Dammit Vernon. Can't you just say thank you?" She snapped.

"Maylan, I don't know what I'm thanking you for or-"

"It doesn't matter. You'll be out of here in the morning. Goodbye." She tried to walk off but I grabbed her arm.

"What do you mean?"

"Vernon, it's done. The situation is handled and right now it's all you need to know. I expected you to be happy."

"You want me to be happy Maylan. You want me to be happy that you went out there doing something stupid instead of waiting? Huh? You want me to be happy that you wouldn't take my calls? Whatever you did, I'm sure it was in the best interest of getting me out, I don't doubt it, but you're so fucking hardheaded. I swear to God you don't listen." I started getting mad, which had me yelling.

"Vernon, I'm not going to apologize for putting my family first. You are my husband and I would do anything for you. If you want to stay mad, then so be it but I don't regret what I did and I would do it all over again to make sure you came home to your son." She wiped her eyes and headed for the door.

"Maylan."

"I don't want to hear it. I heard you loud and clear say I'm hardheaded and don't listen. I'll see you tomorrow."

"Maylan."

"Goodnight Vernon." The guard opened the door for her and just like that she was gone. I went back to my cell and beat myself up in the head about the way I spoke to her. All she was trying to do is get me out of here. I have to make it up to her when I get home. I hate

154

seeing her upset and that's exactly how she left out of here.

Isa

"Mama Isa, do you think Abel will like me?" Brayden asked climbing in the bed with me. I had Ariel on my lap while Katarina and Abel were both knocked out in the middle.

"He's going to love you just like I do." I kissed his cheek and watched him lie back on the pillow. He resembled his father so much; I knew the girls were going to go crazy over him when he got older.

"You love me too."

"Of course I do Brayden. You may not be my biological son but I treat you the same as those two." I pointed to them asleep.

"Just because you're parents aren't together, it doesn't mean no one loves you. People grow apart and find love elsewhere, but it doesn't take away their love for the kids. Honey, Kristopher is your best friend and you know how much he loves his father. I'm sure now that your mom and his dad are together he'll consider you to be his brother the same way Katarina and Abel do. I'll tell you what. Let's invite Abel and your mom to IPlay America one day and you can see for yourself. You never know, you may not like him." I laid Ariel in the crib and sat down.

"I love you mama Isa. If you and my dad ever break up, I'm living here."

"Let your father tell it, we are never breaking up. Do me a favor and don't say that around him. He thinks I'm going to meet Usher and leave him as it is. That's why he won't get me tickets to see him." We both laughed.

I picked Katarina up first and put her in her own bed and did the same with Abel.

Brayden tried to stay awake after our talk but he kept dosing off. I had him go in his room too. I called Birch's cell phone again and he didn't answer. He left out of here a little after six and I haven't seen or heard from him. He told me something went down with Maylan and he had to make sure she was ok.

Instead of stressing myself out over it and thinking the worst, I ran a bath. It felt good to relax and not have anyone yelling or breaking something. These kids were a handful and I couldn't wait until they were older. But I know I'd be missing them even more. I reflected back on the last year and a half and besides the fighting and breaking up I wouldn't change any of it, if I had to do it all over. Birch and the kids are the best thing in my life and with another addition on the way our hands will be full with that and a wedding.

I had gotten out the tub because the person at the time was banging on my door. Had she not screamed for me to open up, I probably would've called the cops.

"Where is Maylan?" Her mom asked when I opened the door.

"She's not here and how do you know where I live?" I asked and she stepped inside, uninvited.

"Who cares how I know? Just tell me where she is. I need this money."

"What did you say?" She kept looking around my house as if she were paranoid or looking for something.

"Are you high?" I asked when I noticed her scratching and the glassy look.

"Mind your fucking business Isa and worry about your own mother whose over in her apartment sucking and fucking for her next hit."

"Come again."

"Oh yea. Why do you think she wanted to get reacquainted with you? Everyone knows your precious Birch has money and so does his friends. If you had let her back in your life she was going to suck you dry. You bitches are with legal, yet, street niggas and still don't know shit."

"Get the fuck out."

"Who you talking to?"

"You, now go before I drag your ass out."

"Mama Isa you ok?" I looked up and Brayden was standing at the top of the steps with his pajama pants on and a wife beater. The next thing out this bitch mouth had me floored.

"Damn whose kid is that? He is handsome. Hey baby you want me to show you a good time?" Brayden was six but taller than normal kids his age but not where she should be trying to fuck him. I snatched her by the back of her hair and swung her around.

"Don't ever come for my son again. I will beat your ass over my kids."

"Bitch, he ain't your-" was all she could get out. I punched her in the face a few times before I felt someone pulling me back.

"What the fuck Isa?" Birch barked at me.

"Get the fuck out bitch and don't ever come back!"

"Yo, aren't you Maylan's mom?" Dante asked holding her.

"Get your hands off me." She spat blood out her mouth. Birch and Vernon had been teaching us how to fight and I'm glad they did because she deserved that ass whooping. I may not be Rhonda Roussey but I handled myself well.

"Tell my daughter Jared is looking for her. Oh and let her know he's coming for that baby in her stomach." She ran out and hopped in some beat up hoopty.

Birch asked me what happened and I could see the aggravation on his face when he heard how she offered herself to Brayden. What kind of woman throws herself at a child? With everything that went down I looked up at noticed Brayden was sitting right next to me. My adrenaline was pumping so much I didn't feel him there.

"Brayden go upstairs." Birch said but he didn't move.

"Are you ok mommy?" My mouth fell open and Birch used his finger to close it. I cleared my throat and told him yes. He gave me a hug and ran up the steps. Dante and Smitty stayed a little longer listening to me tell them what Maylan's mom said. They in return, explained to me what went down with Celeste. I guess tonight is one for the record books. One thing I do know is I had to give my mother a visit.

"I see you put those paws on Maylan's mom." Birch said coming out the shower dripping wet. I know for a fact he did it on purpose because he had no towel wrapped around him and his dick was at attention.

"My man taught me well."

"That he did." He leaned over to kiss me and his dick hit my chest.

"You giving me some pussy or do I have to take it?"

"It's yours to take baby." I pushed him against the wall and gave him what he wanted.

"You ready to marry me yet?" He entered me and stopped to hear my answer.

"Yes baby. Yes." I moaned out and let him make love to me as long as he wanted. I can never get enough of him being inside me.
****

The next day I got up around nine and dressed before Birch. I made breakfast for everyone, fed the kids, made sure they were dressed and headed out the door. The nanny was there watching Ariel because the other kids pretty much took care of themselves. My mission today was to go by my mothers to find out if what Maylan's mom said was true. I called to see if she would ride with me. It would give me time to tell her what happened.

I parked in front of Vernon's mom house and blew the horn. She came out to speak with VJ in her arms. I swear he resembled his father as if he were the one who carried him. Ariel resembled Brayden but you could see me in her as well. No one seems to agree with me on that but I see what I see. His mom told me Vernon was coming home today but that they got into an argument over the incident last night.

"Bye baby." She kissed VJ and hopped in the car.

"Ok. Now tell me everything." She shook her head with disgust listening to me. I felt bad because she wanted her mom to do better but when it's calling you, there isn't much you can do.

I parked in the parking lot of my moms' apartments and we walked up to the door. You could hear soft music playing and a few voices. I figured she was entertaining company. I turned the doorknob to see if it was open and it was. There were some young dudes sitting on the couch smoking and another chick coming out the bathroom barely dressed. I didn't say a word because this isn't my house and I'm sure she knows they're here.

"Who are you?" Maylan asked and one of the guys stood up. He lifted his jeans and came over.

"Damn you sexy." Maylan said to him. I grabbed her hand and took her in the back with me.

"Holler at me when you finished ma." We turned around and he licked his lips.

"Bitch, I don't have time to go to your funeral." She sucked her teeth.

"Girl, I can look as long as I don't touch." I rolled my eyes and knocked on my moms' door. She didn't answer so I opened it and almost threw up.

"WHAT THE HELL?" I yelled out and the only one who made an attempt to move was my mom.

"Nah bitch. If you want this money, you better finish sucking me off until I cum." The one guy said as the other one finished fucking her from behind. My mom shrugged her shoulders and went back to blowing him.

"At least the other dude has a condom on." Maylan said standing there.

159

"Isa, look how big it is. Your mom sucking the hell out of it too." She was cracking up but I didn't find shit funny. I couldn't even get mad because she's seen her mom do shit worse than this.

"You know what Maylan. I'm out."

"Hold on, I want to see if she swallows." I left out and something told me to go back in there to get her. Lucky I did because the dude from earlier had her backed up against the wall trying to kiss on her neck. *Where the hell did he come from?*

"She's married bro. You're barking up the wrong tree."

"That wet pussy doesn't say she's married." He must've offended Maylan.

"Nigga, you wish you touched my pussy. As far as being wet, not at all. You may be cute but the way you come off is what teenagers do. How old are you anyway?"

"Eighteen why?"

"Exactly! You're a kid."

"Girl you're crazy. Why you let that boy kiss on your neck? Never mind that, how you in there watching my mama suck dick?"

"Isa, ain't you ever heard of watching an OG do tricks to learn new things. Granted, its' your mom but she had that nigga moaning."

"I hate you." I walked out the room and told her I would never return and I meant that shit. I don't know what happened to my mom and the guy she was with and I didn't care. What I do know now is that she's turning tricks with kids and I don't want to be apart of it when child services come up in here.

"Oh shit baby. Fuck me." We heard and opened what used to be my bedroom door. The chick from earlier was fucking some dude on my old bed.

"Your mom having an orgy up in here." We both started laughing and walked out the apartment. Maylan stopped in her tracks and held my arm with her. I asked what was wrong and she pointed across the parking lot where her mom stayed. Her mom was arguing with some dude and from the back I couldn't tell who he was but when he turned around it was Jared. I could feel Maylan's body trembling. I looked at her and she appeared to be terrified. I didn't know what to do so I called Birch.

"Where did you go this early?"

"Babe, I need you to get over here."

"I'm on my way to pick up Vernon. What's wrong?" I started telling him and I could hear the anger in his voice. He hung up and told us not to move. He called me back a few minutes later and said Dante was on his way.

"Relax Maylan."

"Isa, what if he sees me?"

"He won't. Lets go back to my moms' and wait in there." She gave me the side eye.

"We don't have a choice May. Its that or the car and he'll see us if we go there."

"Isa, its not that far. We can make it."

"You're right but what if he follows us. I don't know how to drag race." She laughed at me. I hadn't mentioned to anyone about my pregnancy and right now wouldn't be a good time either, because then she'll be worried about me and I wanted us both to stay calm. We sat down on the steps and waited.

"Hello." I answered when I saw Birch's number.

"You good."

"I don't know Birch. He's still talking to her mom and May is scared."

"Isa baby. I need you to calm down and stay where you are. Dante is about two minutes away from you. Stay on the phone with me."

"Ok." May kept peeking.

"He's going in my moms' house. We can make a run for it." May said and Birch yelled out *"NO"* when he heard her. All of a sudden we heard someone walking towards us.

"Lets go." Dante took the phone from me and told Birch we were going with him and to have someone pick the car up later. The entire ride to my house Maylan was shaking and crying. Vernon had to do something because I hated to see her like this.

Vernon

I could already tell something was up when Birch picked me up from the jail. He had a frown on his face and I could hear him asking the person if they were ok. I assumed it was Isa from the way the rest of the conversation flowed. He stayed on the phone with her for a few more minutes and hung up.

"What up?" We slapped hands and he passed me a black and mild.

"Before I fill you in on what you missed, Celeste has definitely been handled. Your wife was a trooper."

"What you mean?" He started telling me how she basically killed her with a metal bat. I wanted to be mad but how could I, when it was done for me.

"In other news, Jared is still trying to get at her. He's under the assumption Maylan is still pregnant."

"Good. That's going to bring him out." He blew his breath out.
"What?"

"He's mixed up with her mom somehow. Isa went to see her mother about some shit she heard and Jared was outside talking to Maylan's mom."

"Where's Maylan? Is she ok? He didn't get her, did he?"

"Nah. Dante picked them up but I have to stop over there to get Isa's car." I nodded my head and took a few pulls off this mild.

"You good yo?" He asked me as I kept my eyes closed in deep thought.

"Yea I'm good. I'm going to handle him tomorrow. Let me get to my wife and spend time with her." I told him and glanced down at my phone to see if Maylan reached out but she didn't. She was probably still upset over what happened last night when she came to see me.

I didn't mean to take it out on her but if she got caught and locked up, not even Abel could help. At least if I was home, I could take the fall. If she understood the severity of going to jail and being away from VJ, maybe she would've taken me serious.

We stopped by the projects and I hopped in Isa's car. I glanced over by Maylan's mom apartment to see if he was out there but the only people outside were fiends. I pulled out slow, still hoping to run into him but it was no use. I told Birch I had to make a few stops and I would drop the car off later.

My first stop was to see my son. I knew my wife was with Isa and wasn't in a rush to go home. VJ reached out for me as soon as he saw me. My mom had to catch him because he almost fell out her arms. I hugged him tight and kissed his cheek. My mom made me a plate of food from what she cooked last night and told me how Maylan stayed with her the entire time. She also mentioned that my wife kept saying she wanted him dead. My wife has never been in trouble, much less a fighter but she's got her mind set on getting rid of him. I stayed at my moms most of the afternoon talking to her and Mike.

"Alright ma. Let me go get my wife." She kissed VJ goodbye and walked us to the car.

I hopped in Maylan's car and strapped my son in the car seat. I told Birch to drive Isa to pick the car up since I couldn't drop it off.

I pressed the button for the garage door to open and parked inside. I smelled food cooking and stepped in the kitchen. Maylan didn't see me so I slipped out and put VJ in his walker and turned the television on. He was content for the moment sucking on the pacifier. I walked back in the kitchen and kissed the back of her neck.

"I'm glad you're home baby." She turned around with glassy eyes and jumped in my arms. I thought she was still mad at me but I guess not.

"I told you I was coming home." She slipped her tongue in my mouth and fiddled with the button on my pants until she was able to get them undone. I lifted her up, pushed my way in and stopped.

"Why you stop Vernon?"

"It's been a few weeks May. I almost came." She found it to be funny. I felt her body moving and just that fast, let go.

"You were serious?" Now she had an attitude.

"You play too much. I said give me a minute to hold it in." I put her down and pulled my clothes up.

"Where you going?"

"To lay down. I'm tired May."

"You weren't sleeping in there." She walked to the stove.

"How can I, when my wife was out in the streets playing Wonder Woman."

"Vernon-"

"I'm over it. I'll be down when I get up. VJ is in the living room." I went upstairs, took a quick shower and got in bed. It was five thirty and I just wanted to take a quick nap. I woke up and Maylan was next to me asleep. The time on my phone said two in the morning. I went to check on my son and use the bathroom. I came out and my wife tossed the covers back revealing some lingerie set she had on.

"I thought you were sleep." I said smirking

"I was until I felt you get up."

"How do you have that on?" I pointed to the outfit.

"I put it on before going to bed, thinking you would get up. That was a long ass nap." I moved closer to her without responding. My lips found hers and my dick found her opening. I wanted to make love to her but right now the outfit she wore enticed the hell out of me and I didn't want to take my time.

"You do know I'm about to tear that pussy up."

"You better." She wrapped her arms around my neck and dug deep in my back when I began stroking her. I had her in all types of positions and if she wasn't pregnant before, she damn sure is now.

"Vernon, don't ever leave me again." She whispered in my ear and I heard her sniffling. I turned over to see her crying and wrapped my arms around her.

"What's wrong?"

"I missed you Vernon and I was scared he would find me."

"I didn't leave you out here alone May. You might not have known but I had eyes on you. Even when you didn't answer the phone for me, I knew you were in good hands."

"Then why did you yell at me?"

"Because I shouldn't have to call you that many times to answer. I wanted to hear your voice and hear you tell me you loved me. I wasn't playing when I mentioned to you before that I need you in my life."

"You still need me."

"I will always need you Maylan. You and my son have become the reason I wake up in the morning. I didn't want you out here doing something that could take you away from us."

"I'm sorry for not answering your calls and I promise to fill you in next time."

"Yea, well don't do that shit again and it won't be a next time."

"I'm sorry baby." She kissed me.

"Let me not answer and you'll be ready to go off."

"As long as you know." I kissed her forehead and pulled her on top of me to go to sleep.

****

164

I woke up early and got VJ dressed for the day. My mom text me last night and asked if she could pick him up to go shopping with her. She came around ten and asked for Maylan who was still upstairs sleep. VJ whined a little when she took him but he straightened up when he saw Mike in the car. My son is spoiled as hell and my mom and stepdad are partly to blame. I closed the door and went to tell Maylan goodbye but to my surprise her ass was coming out the shower. She let her towel drop and I had to smirk. I knew she was trying to keep me home but I was on a mission.

I lifted the towel up, dried her off and handed her one of my t-shirts. No matter what she put on, she was still beautiful. She came towards me and slid her hand in my pants but I backed away. She did a bunch of whining and told me I couldn't leave the house without her. I was about to say something but her phone started ringing and she showed me who the caller was. I told her to answer it and put her on speaker.

"Yes, mother."

"Maylan. I didn't think you would answer. How are you?"

"I'm fine mother."

"Are you really? I know your husband is in jail and you're most likely lonely." I put my finger up to let her know, not to tell her I'm home. If she believes I'm in jail, she's up to something.

"I'll manage. What are you calling me for?"

"Does a mother have to have a reason to call her daughter?"

"You do. The last conversation we had, you disrespecting my husband and then went to Isa's house and tried to sleep with her stepson." I couldn't believe what I was hearing and caught an attitude off that shit. Birch, must've forgot to mention it but then again we discussed so much it probably did slip his mind.

"That's in the past. Why don't you come by and visit?" I saw her eyes get big.

"Hold on ma. Somebody is on the other line." She put the phone on mute.

"Tell her ok."

"I don't want to Vernon. What if she-"

"Do you trust me May?" She shook her head yes.

"Just tell her what I said and leave the rest to me." I sent Abel a text and asked if he got what I needed. Once he said yes, I told Maylan to tell her she'd be there around one. She hung the phone up and stared at me. Birch and I came up with a plan yesterday but he had

165

to get Abel involved because he knew a lot more people than us.

"I'm taking you to Birch's house." I handed her some clothes to put on and waited for her to get ready.

"Vernon, be careful please." She got dressed and followed me down the steps. We turned everything off in the house, locked up and were on our way.

The ride over all I could think of was getting this nigga and put him out of his misery but as promised, I could only whoop his ass. The deal I made with Abel was to get him to some warehouse, beat his ass and save his death for him. It's probably because he found out Jared is the one who got him knocked at Isa's. I planned on staying there to watch him take his last breath though. I needed to see it myself and let my wife know for sure he won't ever come back.

"You ready."

"Yup. May let me get your phone." She handed it over without as much as a why.

"Vernon please stay in touch with me." I handed her my phone.

"If I don't text you back right away, I'm busy but I will have Birch stay in touch with Isa." She nodded her head and kissed me.

"I love you Vernon."

"I love you too."

"Lock the door Isa and Smitty will be over with Maria and the kids shortly. He's going to call you before he comes." He kissed her and we headed out to the car. His phone rang from Abel and he told him I didn't have mine but we were on the way.

We parked in the parking lot of the apartments but further in the back. I got out and threw the hoodie over my head with Birch doing the same thing. It was cloudy out and not too many people were strolling the streets. We made it to Isa's moms' complex and waited for the chick to come. We could see Maylan's mom apartment from where we sat.

Abel had found one of the chicks who worked for him that resembled Maylan. All I needed her to do was go into the complex looking as if she were paranoid and knock on her moms' door. Nine times out of ten Jared was there or her mom was going to call him.

"You Vernon." Some chick asked behind us. I turned around and the girl was definitely pretty and resembled my wife. She had the long hair, her body was petite and she wore clothes similar to what

May would. She had a cap on her head and some black Timbs on her feet. Shorty was gangsta as hell and I felt bad for Maylan's mom because I was having this chick beat her ass, if I found out she set this up for Jared to get my wife.

"What up? Thanks for doing this."

"No problem. Abel, is my peoples and I know all about Jared."

"You do."

"Yup. He came into town trying to sleep with my sister. He tried to sleep with her the first night they went out and when she wouldn't, he choked her. My brothers tried to find him but he disappeared."

"Damn, he was really trying to get these women out here."

"I know. What do you need me to do?" I explained everything to her and she happily obliged. Shorty removed her nine out her waist and cocked it. I guess she wasn't taken any chance and I don't blame her.

She walked over to Maylan's mom spot and kept looking back and around the complexes as if she were scared. Now, from behind she was a spitting image of my wife but you wouldn't know she wasn't until you got up on her.

All of a sudden a male figure began walking in her direction being just as paranoid. You could see him watching her and tried to keep his distance. Birch and I made our way over and heard him yelling an asking who she was. He came running out and straight into me. I hooked off on him and put that nigga straight to sleep.

Birch pulled the car around and two of Abel's men that came in a black van, picked him up and tossed him in the back. I asked them to wait a few minutes because I needed to handle something. I called Maylan as me, the chick and Birch walked up to her moms' apartment. I banged on the door and waited for her to answer. Her smile turned into a frown when she opened it.

"Hello mother." Maylan said on the face time. I told her if we found out her mom was involved she was getting her ass beat and she agreed. I pushed the door open and turned the phone to face her.

"You set your own daughter up to get a fix."

"Maylan, he was going to kill me and-"

"I don't want to hear shit. Once again you chose those drugs over your child and now you have to pay. Vernon, make sure she doesn't take it easy on her but don't kill her. I want her to feel the pain and suffer for months like I did, after what that asshole did to me."

After she said that, I hung up and gave a head nod to the chick who wasted no time rocking the hell out her. Maylan's mom tried to fight back but she was no match for the beat down she received. By the time she finished, her mom was barely breathing. We left out and went to handle the motherfucker who tried to kill my wife. Shorty rode behind us in her car. I promised her a few hits for her sister. It's the least I could do for helping me. She wouldn't take any money from us nor did she plan on fighting.

"Wake up motherfucker." I threw a bucket of water on him. We were in some warehouse that I'm sure he conducted illegal activities in.

"What the fuck?" He jumped out the chair but I punched him in the ribs and the chick shot his ass in the knee. We looked at her like she was crazy and all she did was shrug her shoulders.

"This is for my wife." I beat the shit out of him until I got tired. He tried to fight back but he had no win over here.

"You finished." I heard Abel say behind me after I kicked him one last time.

"Yea, I'm good. He's all yours but I want to watch. I need to tell my wife I saw him take his last breath."

"Not a problem." Abel put on a pair of plastic gloves someone handed him and lifted Jared up by the shirt.

"Abel, you're going to let him do this to me?" He said barely above a whisper.

"You did this to yourself." He didn't say anything.

"Before I end your life, just tell me why you thought it was ok to snitch on me?"

"Abel-"

Phew, Phew, Phew, Phew! Abel didn't even allow him to answer before he took his life in front of us. His brain was splattered all over the floor and you could see he lost his bowels in the process.

"Thanks man. I appreciate you letting me get some sort of revenge for how he did my wife." I told Abel and we slapped hands and did that man hug thing.

"Maylan deserves to be able to walk around without having to look over her shoulder. She's lucky to have you as her man." Birch and I finished talking to him for a few and found out the chick who helped us is his cousin. I swear it's a small world. He didn't know about Jared doing that to her sister but once he did, he became a target for him as well. The crazy part is Jared had been hiding from Abel for a while and

Abel didn't know why, but he does now.

"Thank you so much baby." Maylan said when we got home, showered and were lying on the couch chilling.

"I'll do anything for you Maylan Davis."

"And I'll do anything for you Vernon Davis." She moved up my chest and pecked my lips. Our love is forever and ain't nobody ever taking her from me again.

Epilogue
1 Year later

I sat on the chair in the middle of the floor, staring at the two women dance for me at my bachelor party. I promised Isa that my hands wouldn't touch another female but these chicks in front of me made it hard as hell. They both had big titties and their ass was jiggling to the beat. One of them leaned over and all you saw was her pussy. I bit down on my knuckles and continued to look without touching.

When the song was over I stood up and let another dude get the treatment. There's no way in hell I could sit through another set and not want to touch. The bartender passed me a beer and a shot. I wasn't trying to get too drunk because having a hangover at my wedding is not a good look and I would never hear the end of it.

"So you're getting married huh?" I turned around and it was Lira. How the hell did she know about this?

"Goodbye Lira."

"Come on Birch. Don't you want one last chance to get your dick wet before you walk down the aisle?" She had this dumb grin on her face.

"Not at all." I nodded my head and security came over and tossed her out. I told him no other females were allowed in here. I'm not even sure how she snuck in. I took a seat at the bar and watched all the dudes out there having the time of their lives with the strippers, including Dante, who got married a week after Vernon came home from jail. Dawn refused to have another baby by him and they weren't married. I think it made her parents happy too. You know parents want their kids to be married before they have kids but it doesn't always work that way.

Vernon and Maylan were at peace with their ex's being out of their life. Two days after the shit with Jared, she went to the doctors and he told them she was expecting. She gave birth to their daughter two months ago and they just found out she's pregnant again. He wasn't playing when he said he would keep her barefoot and pregnant. Maylan told him she was getting on birth control because she is not going to have a baby every year. Of course, he ignored her.

Maylan, asked Vernon to put her dad in one of the condos or apartments and he did. Her father was now working and dealing with some woman he worked with. He still attended his meetings and

170

sometimes Maylan would go with him. Her mother passed away from an overdose four months ago. She wasn't upset and didn't have a service for her.

Smitty and Maria are doing fine and so are the kids. They received a few phone calls from Edie here and there threatening them. I say, they because she talked shit to Maria too. That woman is some kind of crazy. She won't step foot back in town but if she did Maria would be right there waiting.

Barry stayed out in California but as you can see anytime something popped off, he'd be right here. He isn't as violent as the rest of us, but nonetheless he is our boy and always had our back.

He met some chick about six months ago and brought her to meet us and she seemed nice. Barry had his hands tied with her though. This woman played no games and watched his every move. We told him he better get rid of her because if she's a stalker now, she'll be a lunatic later.

Lique had a daughter by Abel and the two of them got married in the Bahamas, shortly after. It was just those two and to be honest, he appeared to be the one who was able to get her to calm down. Brayden says she is doing better with her mommy duties but that Isa will forever be the woman who he connects with.

Isa will let Lique know when she's messing up and it's usually when he's here with us. She won't call him everyday to check up on him or the weekends he stays over with her, he always asks for Kristopher to stay. I try and stay out of it because she has to deal with that. As far as Abel, well, we all squashed the beef we had with him and we're back to normal. He stays out of our way and vice versa.

Isa and her mom never spoke again after she witnessed the orgy go down. Child services was contacted and she went to jail for having sex with minors. Isa didn't feel bad at all and laughed when she heard. The guy her mom kicked her out for those years ago is now in jail for child molestation. He snuck in some kids bedroom, molested the little girl and the father walked in and beat him half to death and then called the cops to come get him.

These last few years have been pretty hectic but I wouldn't change anything because then my soon to be wife and other kids wouldn't be here.

I took my phone off my hip since it was vibrating and saw it was Isa texting me. I opened the message and had to go in the bathroom. She had the phone sitting on the dresser of our bedroom as she pleasured herself and called out my name. I thought about sending her one back but this wasn't a private bathroom and I didn't need anyone barging in. I was definitely going to handle that tomorrow after the wedding. I cleaned myself up, washed my hands and opened the bathroom door.

"What were you doing?" Vernon asked leaning on the wall outside.

"Nothing motherfucker. Why you all up in my business?"

"Whatever. Look at Dante's drunk ass. That nigga about to go home smelling like pussy and Dawn is going to kick his ass out. Make sure you open the door for him." I looked over and one of the strippers had her breasts in his face and he was smacking her ass.

"Why can't he come to your house?"

"Shittttttt. I'm about to call my wife up, have her meet me outside and get some pussy in the car." He tilted his beer back and had a stupid grin on his face.

"You trying to be funny." He shrugged his shoulders.

"I know you and Isa's nasty ass probably fucked all day and sent each other some freaky ass videos. You now have eight hours to walk down the aisle and then you can be all up in them guts." I sucked my teeth and left him standing there. I felt someone tug at my arm and turned around to see my future wife.

"You do know you're not supposed to see the groom before the wedding." Vernon said.

"Well, maybe I should tell Maylan to go back to the hotel. It's not good for the matron of honor to come out in just a robe to see her husband either. But let me text her." She pulled her phone out and Vernon hauled ass out the club.

"Come here Brayden and let your fiancé fuck you one last time before walking down the aisle." She grabbed my hand and we went into the bathroom. I waved for one of the security guys to come over an asked him not to allow anyone access in here. I closed the door and Isa opened the jacket she had on and revealed the black fishnet stockings with some black pumps. The one-piece lingerie she had on made my dick stand straight up.

"Damn baby. I'm glad you came." I walked over to her.

"What can I say? I'm Addicted To Loving A Boss."

"Oh, I'm a boss huh?"

"At work you are." She kissed my lips and started unbuttoning my jeans.

"At home you are." She placed a few kisses on my neck and let my jeans fall.

"You are definitely the boss in the bedroom." She put more kisses on my stomach and removed my boxers.

"And when you're inside me, you are the boss of my body."

"Oh Shitttttttt. Isaaaa." I grabbed hold of the sink to keep from falling when she took all of me in her mouth. This woman had my toes curling in my Jordan's and my eyes rolling. I loved watching her swallow and she knew it because she'd stare up at me, like she's doing now and suck me dry. I helped her up off the floor and kissed her hard.

"Bend that ass over and let this boss fuck the shit out of you."

"Oooh yes daddy. Give me all that dick." And that's exactly what she got. When we were done she called Maylan's phone to tell her she was on her way out. She didn't want to walk in on them doing what we just finished. I kissed her and waited for them to pull off. I was content for the last hour of being here after getting my fix. All I had to do now was meet Isa at the altar and nothing was stopping me from doing it.

****

"Are you happy Mrs. Glover?" I asked Isa when we got in the limo and were on our way to the reception.

"I'm very happy Mr. Glover."

The ride over all we did was fondle one another and talk dirty. I wanted to sex her in the limo but she didn't want the driver to see the freaky things she did. The partition was up but she felt like he could still see. I do know once this reception is over, we're joining the mile high club on our way to Turks and Caicos for our honeymoon.

The End...

41608751R00098

Made in the USA
Middletown, DE
18 March 2017